Touchable LOVE

An Untraditional Love Story

By Becky Due

Published by Due Publications

Copyright © 2007 by Due Publications

Library of Congress Catalog Card Number 2007904566

ISBN: 0-9746212-2-6
13 ISBN: 978-0-9746212-2-7

First Edition 2008

Printed in the United States of America

Touchable Love, An Untraditional Love Story is published by:
Due Publications
PO Box 883
Loveland, CO 80539-0883
970-227-4916
www.duepublications.com

Production Credits:
Edited by: Jane Albritton of Tiger Enterprises and
Bevelyn McLise Park of Editors Ink
Layout and Production by: Craig VanWechel of VW Design
Book Cover Photo by: Samantha Jones

You've Got A Friend
Words and Music by Carole King
© 1971 (Renewed 1999) COLGEMS-EMI MUSIC INC.
All Rights Reserved International Copyright Secured
Used by Permission

Dedication:

Touchable Love is dedicated to everyone who has suffered, everyone who is suffering and to all who will love themselves enough to avoid the suffering.

1.

Christy woke up and looked at the clock. It was 2:38am. She grabbed a pillow, pulled the covers up over her shoulders and gently tapped each finger counting how much time she had left to sleep. "2:38 I'll say 3:00… 4:00, 5:00, 6:00, three more hours to sleep." She smiled and drifted off.

When her alarm went off at 6:00am, she didn't press the snooze button. She stiffly rolled out of bed, turned on the hall light and stood in front of the full-length mirror. This morning she expected to see somebody else in the mirror looking back at her. To her surprise, she was still there, only distant and almost unrecognizable. Too many dreams flooded her sleep, and she woke unsure of what they meant.

Christy couldn't wait to leave Minnesota. She had never been to Florida, and she felt so professional getting on a plane for a job interview: first-class airfare and hotel paid for by her – fingers crossed – future boss. She had to win him over, and she had three days and two nights to do it. She wanted this job more than anything even though she didn't know what the job was. This was it. Her life was changing. But doubts and negative thoughts kept nagging at her.

In Miami, the heat and humidity enveloped her as soon as she stepped out of the airport. She stood in line waiting for a cab and listened to all the languages. She liked Florida.

Christy stood at his door knocking. She was anxious to see him, to see more of his work. She could hear painful coughing on the other side of the door. She hoped she wouldn't catch his cold.

The door opened and there stood a thin, sickly looking man. "Christy?" he asked.

"Yes. Paul?" she asked back, hoping it wasn't.

"Yes. Come in." He coughed again and stepped aside to let her in.

She hesitated then stepped into his place. He closed the door and she followed him down the dark hallway into the kitchen. His jeans and t-shirt were hanging off him like he was nothing more than a skeleton with clothes.

"How was your flight?"

"It was good. This is my first time in Florida. It's so warm… and green."

"Can I get you something?"

"No, I'm fine." Christy didn't want his germs.

She was feeling uncomfortable and wanted to leave. She regretted letting him fly her to this interview. She didn't expect this. "Listen... if this is a bad time?" she asked hoping for a way to escape.

"There is no such thing as a bad time for me, only little time."

She was too afraid to ask what he meant and followed him into his studio. He sat down at his desk, and she sat on the black leather couch by the painted brick wall. She set her bag next to her and uncomfortably looked around as he watched her. The large, open room was loaded with cameras on tripods, lights, backdrops, fans and props. In the office area where they sat, much of his famous work was framed and hanging on the brick wall.

"So you're into photography?" he asked.

"Beginner, but yes."

"Did you bring some of your work?"

"No, I didn't bring anything. I wanted to meet you to start with. I left it in my hotel room."

"It doesn't matter. Craig sent me your portfolio. Not bad, for no education."

Christy hid her anger at Craig for not asking her if he could send her portfolio and at Paul for his education comment.

"Craig speaks highly of you. He said you are the best model he's ever had, but wondered why you stayed working as a nude model for so long. He believes you should be the one creating the art, not being the art. So here's your chance... what do you think?"

"I'm not sure," she said, then added, "I do love your work."

He stared at her for a moment and was impressed she didn't look away. "What do you think is wrong with me?" he asked.

She stared back and didn't answer.

"Good answer," he said and coughed. "You're right, I have AIDS."

Christy's heart sank. She didn't want to hear it, and especially didn't want to be around this man. It wasn't pain he was in, it was anger and she didn't want to deal with it. He talked to her like he hated her, and he didn't even know her.

"And I'm gay. My partner died three years ago. And I have, oh... one to five months to live." He coughed again. "Now what do you think?"

"I think you've given up," Christy said.

He started laughing. Then suddenly serious he said, "Fuck you, Christy!"

Christy grabbed her bag and stood to leave.

"Don't go... I didn't mean it. You're right. I've given up. I'm ready to go, to be with him again."

"Your partner?" Christy asked and sat back down.

"Yes, I miss him. I miss company."

"There are so many groups and support. Don't you..."

"Yeah, yeah! I know! No, I don't! I have nothing in common with any of those people except that I'm dying of AIDS. Besides, I'm not a group kind of guy."

"Neither am I," Christy agreed.

He smiled at that. "You're very pretty, Christy."

"Thanks, but I'm not here to model."

"I know. I am," he said.

"What do you mean?"

"Christy, I'll teach you everything I know. I'll introduce you to all the right people and give you all my equipment when I go in exchange for a few things."

"What are you talking about?"

"I want you to record me dying of AIDS. When I'm gone, I want the book of photos published and to be available everywhere. I may do some writing along with it. I'm not sure. I want the book handed out at bars, malls and street corners, everywhere. I have enough money to cover all costs and any money made from this book must go to AIDS research. Christy, you won't make much money from this. Just what I pay you, but when it's over you'll be famous and a working photographer until you retire. I can promise you that."

Christy listened with a knot in her stomach. She was willing to take it on — not for the fame, equipment or connections, but for the opportunity to be a part of something so important. Her own fears reminded her that even if it was too late for Paul, it wasn't too late for so many others, including herself.

"Am I to move in with you?"

"You'll have to, to capture important moments. Christy, you'll be with me all the time."

"As a nurse?"

"Well, I may need help in time. What you can do I'd appreciate, but if it gets too tough I'll hire a nurse to finish it out. I'm not going to a hospital anymore." He turned away, coughed and said, "You know, there's risk involved, not a lot, we'll be very careful but..."

"My whole life's been a risk. I'll do it."

2.

Christy quit modeling and her job at the art gallery; she was planning to be out of her apartment within three days. She didn't have a lot of possessions, but the apartment was full of memories. She was ready to leave her past behind.

She had moved in when she turned twenty-one. It was a new chapter in her life — she had become an adult and could now legally drink and go to bars. She couldn't wait to party and have lots of sex with lots of different men. Christy was wild. Nobody could tame her. The men who tried, the ones who cared about her, would lecture her. She'd listen and smile. She loved it; she loved the lectures. She wasn't sure why. Maybe it was the attention she got, all their energy focused on her. It didn't do any good; she had to live her life.

Christy reached into her closet and pulled out some clothes. A blouse dropped to the floor and Christy was flooded with memories of the last night she wore it. It was on her first date with a man she had met at a bar, a married man. He was easy to be with, no strings, no falling in love. The night they met, they didn't have sex. They just went out for a late night breakfast.

They had a date set up, but she called him to tell him she couldn't make it. It wasn't right.

He called her back to convince her they would have a good time.

She changed her mind and went to the bathroom to blow dry her hair. After, she called him back to cancel.

Again he convinced her to hang out with him — no sex, just friends.

She wasn't that naïve, but agreed. Back to the bathroom to put on her makeup. Then back to the phone to cancel.

He beat her to it. "Yes, you're coming. Now finish getting ready."

She smiled nervously and started getting dressed. She pulled out the blouse from the closet and put it on. Then she took it off and put on her pajamas and reached for the phone. "I'm not coming; don't ask me again!"

"What do I have to do to get you here?"

"Nothing. I'm not coming."

"Christy, I promise we'll have fun. If you're not, you can leave. You can leave anytime you want. Or you can stay with me until it's time I go home. It's your call. What else do you have to do tonight? Come on, let your hair down a little."

Normally, Christy would have already slept with him, but at breakfast he admitted to being married and Christy put the brakes on. She had never wanted to be with a married man before, but he looked nice, smelled nice and dressed meticulously, and Christy figured he had his wife to thank for that.

She went with him that night. And several more nights after that. She always had to drink to be with him; it was the only way she didn't care.

Christy remembered the last night she was with him; he planned to blow three-thousand dollars that weekend. His wife was out of town. He rented a great suite in downtown Minneapolis. Their days would be filled with sex, and the nights with bar hopping.

His wife called his cell while they were in the hotel bed trying to decide what to order for lunch. He panicked. He had to go home. He'd be back later. "Enjoy the room, the room service. There's plenty of beer in the fridge. Have fun. I'll be back by 6:00 tonight."

Christy drank a lot of beer and felt sorry for herself and felt sorry for his wife. By the time she mustered up the decency to leave, she was too drunk to go. Besides, she knew if it wasn't her, it would be somebody else. He had told her all his stories, all the women, all the cheating and lying. Christy had nothing else to do.

She planned that close to 6:00pm, she would get into the big bathtub. She fantasized that he'd come in and find her beautifully soaking in the tub with a beer — it would be a moment he'd remember. And he would want her and wonder why he left in the first place.

When 7:00pm came and went, Christy got out of the tub, naked and shriveled.

It was dark outside. Two of the walls of the suite were solid windows with the drapes wide open. She didn't care, she was up so high only cleaning staff from the adjacent office buildings would be able to see her. She found the stereo and a CD of romantic piano music. She popped it in. She reached for her beer, but it was empty. The heat from the bath and the beer was catching up to her. Her head felt full and her walking seemed staggered. She tried to convince herself she was just walking in a romantic way, matching the music. She made her way to the fridge and grabbed another beer. She stood next to the floor-to-ceiling windows and felt the cool glass. She looked down at all the lights and the cars and boats filled with people. She wondered where they were all going. She wondered if one of the cars was Bob trying to get back to her, but she doubted it.

"Twenty-eight storys," she said out loud, still looking down. "Well, I have more than that! Story after story after story... Will you ever grow up!" she shouted. Christy pushed her bottle of beer against the window making a loud clang, then quickly checked for cracks. "It's OK. Wow! The only thing keeping me in is this thin piece of glass." She laughed, and then thought, "Maybe I should just end my misery."

She slowly paced along the window rubbing her shoulder against the glass. She stopped in the middle of one pane and pressed her naked body against it. She felt like she was lying on a cold, transparent bed hanging over the city. She closed her eyes and wished the bed would give way and she would fall into the twinkling stars below. She started to fall and opened her eyes; she wasn't falling. She turned around and slid down the glass wall until she was seated on the floor still leaning against the window. Suddenly, she wanted to be in her own apartment, in her own bed. She crawled to the bed and started collecting her things. She opened the bedside drawer and saw the Bible. She picked it up and looked at it. "God is in every hotel room... spying on us. The good people rest easy. The bad people are restless." She wondered if she should take it. She was an adulterer and she was restless. She called the front desk to get her a cab. They couldn't understand her slurs, so she had to repeat it three times.

Haphazardously carrying her things, she walked barefoot to the lobby. She was certain her shoes would make her fall. Her hair was still damp and unbrushed. Her pajama bottoms were inside out and her t-shirt was on backwards, but she thought people were staring at her because she was extremely sexy.

All she could think of was that she had to get home.

Christy argued with the cab driver about picking her up in a few hours so she could go and get her car. She didn't want her car to be left alone. She claimed to be an unfit mother leaving her car. She refused to get out of the cab until he promised to come back and get her. So he promised.

Christy slept until 1:30 that afternoon. When she woke up SG, her sexual service guy, was knocking on her bedroom window. She got up, let him in, then made her way to the couch.

"What's goin' on? I tried to call you all last night and this morning." He turned and hit her answering machine, expecting to hear his voice. But it was Bob.

"Christy, I'm sorry it took me so long. Why'd you leave? Come on pick up! At first I thought you went out without me, but then I saw all your stuff was gone... come on, Christy, I'm sorry."

The next two calls were from her service guy.

Then another one from Bob. "Christy, I have this room for two more nights. Please come back. I'll be waiting to hear from you, room twenty-eight-ten."

That was enough for SG. He deleted all the calls on the machine and headed to the kitchen. He came out with a wet towel and a glass of water. He adjusted the pillow behind Christy's head as she took a drink of water. Then he placed the cool towel across her forehead.

"This is your fault for ditching me."

"Screw you!" she said softly with her eyes squinting. "I didn't ditch you!" She held onto the cool towel as if pushing it into her headache. "What are you doing here?"

"What do you think?" He smirked.

"Give me a ride to get my car."

"Where is it?"

"Downtown."

"What will you give me if I do?"

"We could have a threesome with the guy I ditched last night."

"… two guys and a girl… not my thing. But you go, have fun."

"I'm not going; I was joking. Just take me to get my car, or I have to take a cab."

"All right, let's go. Do you need a shower?"

Christy looked at him like, duh… "but I'm not taking one. I just want to get my car out of there."

As they were headed to his car, he asked, "How about I pick up a movie tonight?"

"Sure."

She thought about SG. He was never in a relationship and always available. She used to have so much fun with him. She smiled then laughed about how she would always get pissed at him for some reason, usually because he was trying to smother her, and he would always steal something from her apartment. To get it back, she'd have to call him again. She always did. He was fun and sexy and sometimes she would go and listen to him play the piano and sing late at night in an empty hotel lounge.

The phone rang and brought Christy out of her past. She wadded up the blouse of bad memories and threw it in the garbage. She plopped down on her chair by the closet and answered the phone. She hung up on the telemarketer. She held the phone and tapped it against her cheek trying to remember SG's phone number because she wanted to call and say good-bye, even though she hadn't talked to him for over a year. After Christy quit having sex he quit calling. He'd call once in a while to see if she was having sex yet.

"Hello."

She recognized his voice. "SG, how are you?"

"Christy, how are you? Wow, it's been a while. You must have heard the news… yep, I met the woman of my dreams. We're engaged."

"Wow!" Christy said. "I didn't hear the news. But congratulations! That's wonderful!" Christy's guts turned. "I'm in shock!"

"You must have fallen off the celibacy wagon?"

"What? Oh, no! I'm still waiting for Mr. Right. No, I was calling to say good-bye because I'm moving to Florida for a job."

"Hey, that's great. I guess we both get to celebrate… for you it's celebate!" he chuckled. "Thanks for calling."

"So how did you meet?" The phone was quiet. "Hello… Hello…"

Christy hung up the phone and tossed it onto the bed. "Wow." She didn't know what to think or how to feel.

Christy realized she hadn't known how to feel for a long time when it came to men. She remembered breaking into a man's house because she thought he was cheating on her, but they weren't in a relationship. She sat in his place waiting for him to come home; when he didn't, she took all his clothes out of his closet and drawers and threw them on the floor. She stomped on his clothes for a while before realizing she didn't even want to be in a relationship with this man.

Another time, Christy went to a party and found herself surrounded by old flings. But there were fresh new guys, and she was anxious to hook up with one of them. Unfortunately, one of the more recent guys she had been with must have thought that if you sleep with Christy, you own her. While Christy was standing close to her new conquest, talking and laughing and making plans for the night, she was suddenly thrown against the wall in front of everyone. Wanting to protect her new conquest, she told him to walk away even though he tried to protect her from the other guy. Christy didn't even see it coming. She left with her new conquest's phone number, but she was humiliated and painfully holding back the tears. She had to keep her pride.

Over the years there were other guys who were good, decent men actually wanting a relationship with her. Some even talked about marriage and kids, but Christy ran from those men.

Then she remembered the guy from the gym. Christy assumed he was gay or he was only interested in her as a friend because he never really hit on her or asked her out. The longer that went on, the more she wondered. They used to go to movies together, out for breakfast or lunch. He even went so far as to get involved in her personal life and lecture her. Christy was very attracted to him and always wondered if they might end up together, married with kids. When he asked her out for dinner, her expectations were high that he wanted to go out with her, start dating her exclusively. But no, he just wanted to admit that he had a list of three women and he was trying to decide who he would seduce. Well, he had found God so he wanted to confess to all three of them.

That one really mixed her up. She would have loved to have had sex with him, he should have let her know… and the whole time she thought he respected her and genuinely cared about her.

Christy lay on her mattress and thought about all her one-night stands; they were all one-night stands. When Christy drank, she was careless about sex and about her company. Her life at certain points was a blur. She remembered the bad things she did, but not who she did them with. That's what scared her the most.

Christy thought about the last time she had sex and couldn't believe it had been two years now. A one-night stand had changed her life. He was young, tall, extremely sexy with dark hair, tan skin, green eyes, not too muscular. He was beautiful. After they had sex, she could tell he wanted to go to sleep. So she nudged him and told him, "Either go, or go again." He decided to go again. Again, he wanted to go to sleep, but she repeated, "Either go, or go again." This time, he decided to go.

After he left, she thought, "Good riddance. I have the bed to myself." She grabbed her remote and turned on her stereo. "Bridge over Troubled Water" was playing. Suddenly the song stopped and a man's concerned voice interrupted the silence. "Breaking news, what a sad day this is for everyone. It has been confirmed that Princess Diana has been killed in an automobile accident. We will bring you more details as we…"

Christy began to cry. The tears were a mixture of sadness for Princess Diana and for herself. But the mixed-up feelings came from being alone, and she couldn't understand why she felt lonely. Was it because she made him leave? No, it couldn't be. Christy had always been alone, even when her mother was alive. Was it because Princess Diana reminded her of her own mother dying?

Her one-night fling called her during the week and wanted to see her again the next weekend. One-night stands often did, but she didn't like to see them twice and let any attachment develop at all. But he was young, and she figured there would be no chance for a relationship. If she remembered right, he was going away to school, so she agreed to see him again.

After they had sex the second time, he did a simple thing that changed her life forever. They were lying next to each other with her back facing him. Thinking she was asleep, he put his warm hand on her shoulder, then reached for the covers and gently covered her.

That night, he spent the night.

For the first time Christy had a taste of what it would feel like to have a relationship. To love somebody, to be loved by somebody.

Christy stopped spending time with SG, stopped the one-night stands and stopped dating. She still avoided closeness with men, but for a different reason. She was afraid of the possibilities.

Once Christy stopped having sex, her life got easier in many ways. She was bored sometimes and remembered the parties and bars and fun nights and days. But she didn't have to wonder so much about men because she kept them as friends only.

Her life had been a blur filled with chaos and as destructive as it was, it was what she knew. And now, she had just quit everything to start a new life, a new job, and she was scared shitless.

3.

At Paul's, Christy had the upstairs to herself. It was more like a loft with a large open room and a private bath. It had been Paul's room, but he moved downstairs when it became difficult for him to get around. The move, the change, had been very stressful for Christy. "What if I can't pull this off? This is too important to let such a beginner take on." And like everybody else, she was afraid of AIDS.

Christy was in her bathroom putting towels away when she heard the buzzer, an intercom system installed for Paul in case he needed her. "Christy!" She ran down the stairs and into the studio, grabbed the first camera she saw and took off down the hall to his bedroom. He wasn't there. "Paul!" she yelled.

"Bathroom," he moaned.

She opened the bathroom door. He had his eyes closed lying with his face against the seat of the toilet. Blood and vomit covered part of his face and most of the toilet, even where his face was lying. There was vomit down his shirt and on the white floor tiles.

She held up the camera and started shooting. She felt heartless not offering him help, not asking if he was OK, not calling an ambulance. He was so still she wondered if he was dead. Her eyes blurred but she kept shooting, tears rolling down her cheeks. She wiped them with the sleeve of her sweatshirt. Her nose began running with her tears, and she wasn't sure if it was from the smell or crying.

When Paul heard her sniffing, he opened his eyes and saw her crying. He left his head lying and said, "Christy, I'm OK." He quickly turned his head and threw up again. Christy kept shooting the pictures, and crying.

Between Paul's heaving, he tried to talk to Christy. He told her she was doing a great job. "How's the lighting?" he asked. "Maybe you should grab some of the smaller lights... You... can hook them to the towel bar or shower... Is the... light from the window causing... problems? Try closing the... blinds and take a few."

Christy's tears stopped when she ran to get the lights. She was mixed-up wondering if it was too late for her and she was in hell. She could see her future. She stood outside the bathroom trying to get a grip, not believing any of what was happening. She wanted to pound her head against the wall and pray for God to take her away.

"Christy."

The bathroom was large enough she was able to step around him and close the blinds. She hooked the light on the towel bar and threw a light towel over it to dim the brightness. She began shooting from the back. His dingy white t-shirt, wet from sweat and sticking to him, revealed his thin body lying against the toilet, still covered in vomit and blood. His bathroom, in shades of whites, created a brilliant contrast. "Paul, do you have any black and white?"

"Yeah, in the camera on my desk."

Christy ran out and grabbed it. When she came back, he was vomiting again. She quickly stepped to his back and began shooting again. "Can you take your shirt off?"

"If you grab some gloves from the drawer and help me."

Before he finished, Christy had the gloves and was putting them on. She gently touched his back and he sat up a bit, lifting his arms. She pulled his shirt over his head and began crying again. She had never seen someone so thin and sick. She threw the shirt aside and placed her hand on the back of his head to straighten his hair. The warmth from his head reminded her that he was a human being just like her, that he was some mother's baby.

"Pictures!" he ordered.

Taken away for a moment, Christy pulled off the gloves, picked up the camera with the black and white film and cried while taking the pictures. She could see his skeleton so clearly. He began gagging again, but this time it was only dry heaves.

Christy alternated cameras. His yellow skin was turning reddish from the pain of heaving, his face, neck and shoulders were red from pressure.

"Let me get you some water!" Christy started to put the camera down.

"N... No! Keep shoo... ting!"

"No!" Christy yelled. "This is enough!"

When she came back from the kitchen, he was shivering and very pale again. Handing him the water, she asked, "What should I do? A blanket, do you want a blanket?"

"No. Turn on the water... bath. Warmer than luke... not hot."

Christy did as asked.

"Camera!" he demanded.

Christy grabbed it. "Got it!"

Paul, still shaking and very unsteady, began to remove his pants.

Christy backed up to get his full naked body, but the pain on his face received most of the attention. She lay down on the floor and kept shooting. He was able to struggle his way into the tub.

She stepped up onto the tub's edge, a foot on each corner, and snapped straight down at him. His head hung low and his body looked slightly deformed from the refraction of the water.

Christy could tell he was beginning to settle. "I'm done," she said.

"Yes. You did good."

"How are you? Can I get you anything?"

"How about a bucket and some rags."

"OK. Where?"

"Kitchen hall closet or garage, I can't remember."

"OK, I'll find them. Can I call someone? A doctor or nurse? You lost a lot here."

"My nurse is Brian. His number is by the phone on my desk."

"OK. Can you reach the buzzer?"

"Yes."

Christy left the door slightly open and brought the cameras back to the studio. Then she picked up the phone and called Brian.

"Brian, my name is Christy, and I'm working with Paul... No. I'm not a nurse, I'm a photographer... Well, he needs you," Christy said, almost breaking down again. "He's been vomiting for about the last hour, with blood, and then the dry heaves. I think he's done for now but he's very weak and pale. I'm scared... OK."

The house sank back into stillness, but not Christy. She collapsed at Paul's desk, her head lying on her crossed arms and her brain frantically searching for answers while a deep ache throbbed in her chest. She had spent the past week and a half with Paul, only being apart when they slept. He had been sick, but nothing like this. She knew it was serious now. He was becoming her best friend… she chuckled at the memory of the first day they met and couldn't believe the bond they had created in such a short time.

Christy went back to the bathroom, but didn't open the door. She stood outside and told Paul that Brian was on his way.

"Come in," Paul said.

Christy opened the door and saw that he was sitting on the edge of the tub wearing a red terrycloth robe. He was clean and the bathroom was clean. Christy was shocked and he could tell.

"I found the bucket under the sink."

"I'm sorry, I forgot."

"No problem. You did fine today. I'm sure you got some good shots."

"Are you better?" Christy asked. "Are you OK? You already cleaned this up? I could have helped, you know."

"No, I'm not better. I'm weak. I just want to go to bed. And Christy, you are not responsible for my messes," Paul said. "But I could use some help getting into bed."

"Sure." Christy stepped up to him and he stood with her help. He wrapped an arm around her shoulder, and she tucked hers under his arm and around his waist. When they got to the bed, she let him sit on the edge while she pulled the covers down for him. Noticing the clock changing to 5:55, she was anxious for Brian to get there.

Paul got into bed and she covered him. "Can I get you anything?" she asked, sitting next to him.

"No... Thank you."

She stood and noticed him shivering under his fluffy down comforter. "Can I hold you?" Christy surprised herself saying it aloud, although she really wanted to.

"What?" Paul asked, but knew what she had said.

"Nothing..." Christy turned to leave the room.

"I'd love it if you would."

Christy turned back and lay on the bed next to him on top of the covers. She held him from behind while he shivered in her arms until he fell asleep.

Christy remembered the many early mornings her mom would come into her bedroom and hold her the same way. Only she always smelled of liquor and men's cologne and the other scent Christy was never sure about until she started having sex. She wondered if she had sex so she could have that smell near her, so she could have her mom near her. Christy started to cry, letting the tears roll down her face, remembering her mom, wishing she were there to hold her, wondering what her mom was thinking about her, if she was watching and proud of Christy or consumed by her own guilt. She wondered if her mom made it to heaven, then wondered if there was a heaven. Christy went to sleep.

4.

Christy woke to Brian coming into Paul's room. He was larger than she expected. Not fat, just big, like a football player. Christy lay next to Paul while Brian hooked up an IV. He put on gloves, then found a vein in Paul's arm and inserted the needle. Paul didn't wake up, or move or flinch.

Suddenly Christy regretted not having the camera and wondered if Paul would be angry. She ran down the hall and grabbed one. As she was looking through the viewfinder at Paul lying so still, so lifeless, Brian turned and saw the camera.

"May I?" Christy asked wanting to get Brian in the photo.

"I don't think you should be taking pictures."

"It's what Paul wants. He's paying me."

He gave her a questioning look.

"I'm telling the truth."

"OK." He turned back to check Paul's blood pressure. Just before he put the stethoscope in his ears he added, "But if you're lying, I'm destroying the film."

Christy grinned and continued shooting.

When Brian was done, he asked Christy to go for a walk with him. They walked down to the end of the driveway and headed toward a park.

"How well do you know Paul?" Brian asked.

"Pretty good, in the short time I've been here."

"You know he doesn't have a lot of time left, right?"

"Yes," Christy answered.

"And did you know it is by choice? He's ready to die."

"No, but do you blame him?"

"He could live longer if he'd take care of himself and take his medication. But he'd rather get sick like this every couple weeks and eventually die," Brian said with disgust. "He won't take any medication until he gets to this point. Then he calls me. I come and medicate him through his IV. I stay with him, take care of him, whatever I have to do. He'll be out for a few days. When he comes to, he feels great. Then it starts all over again. It's been going on for months, close to a year. I can't believe he's still here."

"Well, I don't know. We all have choices, and he's made his. I'd probably do the same thing," Christy said. "Plus, he's doing something really important to help others. That alone is incredible. He's a very strong man. You're not giving him any credit."

They stopped walking. "Look up, Christy!" Brian firmly said. "What do you see?"

Christy tilted her head back. The sky was blue and clear with a couple fluffy white clouds passing by. She could see the tops of large palm trees and an airplane leaving a trail. She was hearing and smelling and feeling the world around her like she had never done before. It scared her. She looked back to Brian. He too was looking up.

"Tell me what you saw," he said.

"Blue sky, airplane..."

"No! What did you see?"

Christy was not sure what he was asking for, but she knew what she saw... God, and that also scared her. She never believed in God, at least not the God she'd been taught to believe in, or the whole Bible thing. But she had always believed in a higher power, and that higher power was looking right back at her today.

"God! Don't you see God?" Brian asked. "And don't you think He would want Paul to fight for his life?"

"Well, first of all, what makes you so sure God is a He? And secondly, I think God gave us the gift of life to do whatever we please with it, and sure, 'God' may be disappointed at times with our choices... but in this case I think 'God' is thrilled with Paul's choice to do what he is doing. And if there is any truth to the Bible, isn't Paul doing what Jesus did. Paul is sacrificing himself in hopes of saving others. His reasons? Who can know for sure, but it doesn't change the fact that he's doing it. And another thing, if you do believe in the 'He God' and all that, why do you care about Paul's life! Doesn't the Bible say his lifestyle is wrong? So maybe you should just be happy to see him go."

"I...," Brian tried to say something.

Christy started crying. "Paul didn't do anything wrong. He doesn't deserve this. Nobody deserves this!"

Brian stepped to Christy and gently gave her a hug. "You know, Christy, our beliefs are closer than you'd think. I'm not sure about you, but I've been programmed and conditioned my whole life to believe certain things. It's hard to break the habit of calling God, 'He'. And about the Bible, we have more proof of dinosaurs than the truth of the Bible, and the Bible doesn't mention them. But one thing I know for sure is that you care about Paul. So do I. So let's make the last of his life great. What do you say?"

"Like what?"

"Well, I've been trying to get him out on my boat all summer. The boat will be on the water for probably the next two weeks, then I'm taking her out to do some work on her before she sells. Let's start there. Let's get him on the boat next weekend. I'll come get you on Saturday morning. We can spend the night there."

Christy was pissed that he kept calling a boat a "she" but she didn't say anything about it. She always remembered men calling their boats and cars "she" and telling her it's because they are high maintenance. But Christy hated it because of the ownership and calling an object a "she." "Sleep on the boat?"

"Well, it's a big boat with bedrooms."

"Wow! That sounds great."

"And I know you see him more and spend more time with him, so could you work on him about prolonging his life?"

Christy gave him a questioning look but didn't answer.

"Just think about it."

5.

Christy had been with Paul for just over two weeks, and she was curious. She wanted to know Paul and his home better. She wanted to know what was behind every door and every drawer. She wanted to be as close to Paul as she could be. Paul kept a lot of his pain inside, and Christy wanted to know more so she decided to snoop around the house while he was resting.

She started in the kitchen to see exactly how he had his dishes organized, what types of food he liked. Inside his pantry, she found a large variety of cold cereal, some with sugar, some with fiber. Christy suddenly jumped back and closed the pantry door. "Oh, my God." She rushed to the drawer with garbage bags and pulled out a thirty-gallon bag, swinging it up and down so the air could open it. As if about to kill the biggest, scariest, most poisonous spider on earth, Christy bravely opened the door and quickly grabbed the box of Lucky Charms and threw it in the garbage bag, panicking, trying to close it while jerking and shaking and running out the front door as fast as she could to the garbage bin out by the street. She threw the bag in and slammed the lid shut, her body quivering with fear. She ran back in the house and closed the door behind her. "OK," she said and took a few deep breaths. She knew it was crazy but since childhood she'd been afraid of that leprechaun on the box.

She decided to look around Paul's office. She sat at his desk and opened the top drawer. There was a photo of Paul and, she assumed, his love, Jim. Christy stared at it for a long time, studying it. She gently touched Paul who was healthier and happier in the photo. She wished she'd known him before. She put the photo on the desk and opened a drawer of folders. The top folder was full of pages and pages of hand-written letters and notes.

My Dearest Love,

You left me several months ago. I can't stand my life without you. I'm miserable. My heart hurts every minute of every day…

Christy thought she heard Paul. She stopped reading and put the folder away. She hurried in to check on him, slowly opening the door to his darkened bedroom. She got close enough to see he was still breathing. It had been hard on Christy helping Brian nurse Paul, changing the IV, checking his temperature, and turning and bathing him.

Christy crawled in bed with him with a warm damp towel. It was late morning and he'd been out for almost four days. She missed him. The bond between them grew stronger everyday, even while he rested. Christy was falling in love with him, not in the traditional sense, but she was feeling emotions she hadn't felt before and she knew it had to be love. She knew she was being selfish, but she wanted him to wake up and talk to her.

She would often go into his room and move around on his bed hoping to wake him, or open his blinds, or make noise. But this morning she lay down next to him and gently sponged him off with a warm towel with no intention of waking him. She noticed he was looking better. Still very thin, but with color in his face, pinks, not yellows. She looked at his facial hair and thought about giving him a shave so when he awoke he'd feel better. He didn't have a lot of facial hair, and it didn't grow at all in certain areas. His cheeks only sprouted a few hairs. His chin and jaw line held most of it. His upper lip was only lightly covered.

Paul was usually still but today she noticed slight twitching. His eyes seemed to be open. She moved closer and saw that he was still asleep. Paul frowned as if he were angry. Christy wondered what he was dreaming about, what went through his mind while he slept. His mouth puckered as if searching for his mother's nipple. Immediately, Christy thought of him as an innocent little baby, so helpless, so dependent. When Paul talked about his mother, it was always positive. Christy began thinking about her. She knew she had to have been an amazing woman. From the photos Paul showed Christy, his mother always held her head high. She supported Paul in anything and everything he was and wanted to be. Paul said it took only one week for her to accept that he was gay. He told Christy she showed up with swatches for redecorating her living room. Christy and Paul laughed until their stomachs hurt over that one. Paul kept the story going by saying she must have gone to the library to read up on gay men or talked to people who told her gay men liked to decorate.

"Well, Paul, I must say, you have an awfully nice place here," Christy winked.

"What can I say, my mom got me interested in decorating."

He was her only child and though she was never ashamed of him, it drove Paul crazy when she would tell her friends that she has a daughter not a son.

"Mom, I'm not a woman; I'm a gay man."

"Oh, honey, they know what I mean. It's just a cute way for me to say you're gay."

Paul told Christy how some of his first clients were his mother's friends. He took family portraits. Word of mouth kept him employed. He said if he had wanted to be a firefighter, his mother would have convinced her friends to set their homes on fire. She was that supportive and believed in him that much. She died before AIDS entered his life.

Christy felt Paul twitch and his eyes opened. He stared at the ceiling as if trying to figure out where he was. He was still and Christy waited for him to move or look around or make a sound, but there was nothing.

"Paul?" Christy gently said.

Paul's head turned quickly in her direction as if she had startled him.

"Hi... How are you feeling? I'm glad you're back. I missed you."

"Christy," he said, as if unsure yet relieved. Tears began to roll from his eyes. "Christy, I'm going to die. I know it... soon. I'm scared."

Christy started crying too, but didn't say anything. She felt it, too.

"That was my time to die. Why didn't I go?" His face was wrenched with pain and fear. The tears were uncontrollable. "Why?"

Again, Christy said nothing but wanted to say it was because he hadn't finished what he started. She leaned back and reached for the camera on the night stand. She wiped her eyes, sat up and started shooting. When Paul heard the first click, he started crying even harder and his hands reached for his face covering it. The sounds stopped, but his body kept shaking. Christy was glad she was using color film because Paul had new and older bruises from where the IV had been inserted in his arms. Some bruises were yellow while others were black.

Christy reached for his arm so he'd move his hands from his face. He did but continued crying, occasionally raising his hands to hide his face.

When Christy felt she had enough shots, she set the camera down and crawled back into bed with him. She held him in her arms while he cried. He clung to her like a lost child finally in his mother's arms, never wanting to let go, feeling safe with her arms wrapped around him. He buried his head in her breast and cried until he fell back asleep.

Christy fell asleep. When she awoke, she gently slipped out of bed and called Brian. She asked Brian to bring over Paul's prescriptions. She told him that Paul changed his mind and was willing to give the medication a try. Brian was ecstatic. He wanted to celebrate, but Christy told him not to make a big deal about it or Paul might change his mind.

Christy paged through the newspaper and came across an article about crystal meth, gay men and AIDS. Paul had been involved in that lifestyle, careless and reckless because of drugs. He had gone to the theaters, parks, bars and parties. He used cocaine and had multiple partners.

Paul always said Jim saved his life, then he killed Jim. Jim came along when Paul was at his lowest. On the surface, Paul's life looked great, glamorous. But it was at night, the after hours, that Paul would sink into the dark hole of drugs and sex. The next morning, he'd have to deal with the fear of what he had done the night before. And by nightfall, he couldn't fight the calling of the drugs. Jim had been one of Paul's models. Paul liked him from the start and not only because he was handsome. Paul liked the fact that Jim wasn't intimidated by Paul's fame. Jim was a down-to-earth, clean-cut guy with morals and values who just happened to be a good-looking gay man. Jim was exactly what Paul needed in his life, somebody on an old narrow gravel country road not in the fast lane.

Paul said he had forgotten about his own values and morals until Jim came along. Jim represented everything Paul wanted to be.

She realized from reading the article that many men were going through the same thing that Paul went through and was still going through. AIDS was on the rise in southern Florida.

She put the paper down and stretched as she reached for the photos she had been taking. Out of the ninety-some recent photos, only a dozen impressed her. Seven of the twelve were color, but it was the black and white pictures that were most impressive. She studied the photos this time, not as a photographer looking at the shadows and lighting, but with sadness, studying his sunken face, dark eyes and fragile body.

"They look great," Paul said.

Christy jumped, shocked to see Paul up and looking so good. He was using his cane.

"How about I make us something to eat? Then we start working on the photos."

"Sounds great. Are you OK? Do you want some help?" Christy asked.

"Sure. I'm weak, but I have an appetite."

Just before they reached the kitchen, the doorbell rang and she knew it was Brian with the medication. She told Paul to start without her and she'd get the door.

"Hi, Brian." She didn't welcome him in for fear Paul would find out about her plan.

"Hey. How's he doing?"

"Great. He's in the kitchen making lunch."

"You're kidding me?"

"No," Christy said, trying to rush him away. "He's looking pretty good. Just remember not to talk about the medication. I think he'd rather keep it quiet."

"Yeah, yeah, I know." He handed her the seven prescription bottles. "The instructions are on each of them, but if you have any questions call me. Paul has all my numbers. I'll be on the boat today. Next weekend is my last weekend with her; she sold. Try to get Paul to come out, OK? We'll spend the night out there, just the three of us."

"Your boat's a she?" Christy asked, kind of pissy. "Does it have anything to do with it being a possession?"

"What? What are you talking about?"

"Never mind… forget it. Make plans because Paul and I will be joining you on your female boat."

Brian smiled and said," When you see it, you tell me if it's a he or a she, OK?"

"OK, I will."

"All right," he said. "I'll pick you guys up Saturday afternoon, probably around one."

Closing the door with her foot to not drop any of the bottles, Christy put them in the top drawer of the table by the door. She picked up one at a time to read the label to see which he should take now, with food. There were four. She closed the drawer and went back into the kitchen, breaking the pills on her way.

"That was Brian. He couldn't stay long. He wanted to know you were OK and to invite us out on his boat. I said we couldn't today but maybe next Saturday."

"What? No! I'm not going out on a boat!" He was upset, like he was up for a fight.

"OK," Christy said. "I'll tell him next time I talk to him."

"OK." He calmed down.

Christy smashed the pills while talking to Paul. "It's supposed to be beautiful next weekend. It's the last weekend he'll have the boat; I guess he sold it." Christy continued talking to Paul's back as he stood at the stove. "We could try to find manatees and dolphins. Wouldn't that be fun? I've never been in a boat on the ocean before. Stuff like that makes me feel such a connection with nature and the earth." Christy scooped the crushed pills into Paul's glass of milk sitting on the table. She stood, grabbed a spoon and some chocolate syrup from the fridge. She stuck the spoon into Paul's glass and continued mixing and stirring the pills. "Oh, and that fresh air," she said with her eyes on him, trying to stir without clanging the spoon. He quickly turned but she was able to put the spoon in her glass before he saw. "What are you doing?" he demanded.

She noticed his milk still spinning and hoped he didn't. She laughed, "It would help if I put the chocolate in first." She squirted a lot in, hoping to distract him from his spinning milk. "I guess I was caught up in the whole boat thing. Do you want chocolate in your milk too?" she asked.

"Sure. That would be nice... but not as much as you." He turned back to the stove.

Christy hated lying to him but she didn't want him to die and leave her.

6.

Occasionally Christy encouraged Paul to go for walks not mentioning the health benefits of walking, but leading him to believe it was because she was bored or wanted to bond with nature.

One afternoon after running a few errands before picking up groceries, Christy said she was having an anxiety attack and asked Paul to walk with her. He seemed worried so he agreed to accompany her.

They walked toward a strip mall before a word was spoken. Christy stopped in front of the party store where they had various colored helium-filled balloons tied to a sale sign on the sidewalk. Looking at Paul expectantly, she asked, "Do you have a little unwanted cash on you?"

"How little?" he asked with a grin.

"Come on!" She grabbed his hand and headed into the store.

Mainly mothers with kids occupied the place. It was bigger than she expected and cluttered with greeting cards, wrapping paper, party games, colored paper, toys, paper plates and balloons. Stopping at the colored paper area, she said, "OK, now we have to agree on one color of paper. Just one sheet."

"What for?"

"Out of all these, which is your favorite color?"

"I like them all."

"Me, too. OK, then let's say, purple is for passion, green is for growth, red is for fire and life, blue is for…"

"Let's use red!"

"Red it is." She grabbed one sheet of the red paper and made her way to the pens. She took a silver lining pen and handed one to Paul, tearing the red sheet in half and giving one-half to him. "Now, you are going to write one problem you have on this sheet of paper that you want to let go of and I'm going to do the same. But we can't tell each other because it's private." Christy looked up and began to tap the pen on her cheek.

Paul laughed at her.

Christy wrote, 'I will let go of my past.'

Paul wrote, 'I will let go of my past.'

She grabbed him by the hand and led him toward the front of the store by the helium balloons. "OK, now we each have to pick a color."

They both said "purple" at the same time, and smiled. Their eyes didn't part. Christy looked away first, then looked back at him again.

He was still looking at her. "Christy, I've never met anyone like you before."

"I've never met anyone like you before either. I love you, Paul."

The sales woman walked over and asked if they wanted balloons.

"Yes," Christy said, "I guess we each want a purple balloon but first can you stick these notes inside?" She asked as they folded them several times.

"Sure."

"We got that paper here so we'll need to pay for that, too… Oh, and we can't mix them up," she said to the cashier.

"I got it, honey."

Christy and Paul drove to a small park with an open sky. They sat down on the bench.

"Paul, I used to do something like this when I worked at the gallery. Whenever we had a big sale, I'd fill helium balloons and tie them to our sign to attract customers. During slow times, I'd stuff little notes inside each balloon before filling them with helium. Then I'd set them free."

"What did the notes say?"

"'If you find this please call Christy' and my phone number."

Paul laughed. "Did anybody call?"

"No."

"Hmm."

"I wonder what I was looking for."

"Maybe you were just lonely."

"Yeah, I guess."

They sat quietly before they let their pasts go.

7.

Christy was lying on the floor in the living room, shirt open, chest exposed for her monthly self-examination of her breasts.

"How old were you?" Paul asked, startling Christy as he walked into the room.

"Eighteen." Covering herself, Christy began feeling nervous in the bright daylight. Had he seen her scars before? Did she look mutilated to him?

"Don't cover up. You look so beautiful." Sitting down at her feet he held her bent legs close to his body to watch her give herself the breast exam. "What do you feel?" Paul asked.

She was flooded with memories of what other people told her she should feel. Her mouth quivered and her eyes filled, the tears sliding down her temple. "I don't know."

"Are you afraid you might find something?"

"No." She felt confident about that. Her left hand started with her right breast. Her fingertips gently pressed into the soft tissue. They felt muscle, bones, scar tissue and numb skin that reminded her of touching something dead. Her tears kept coming. "Sadness."

"Sadness? You feel sadness? Why?" He asked with surprise and sadness in his own eyes, wanting to understand.

How does she describe twenty-eight years of life as Christy into a moment like this? Does she start with the breast reduction, or does she go all the way back to the beginning, being born female? Maybe she should go into her lack of understanding of implants and heavily padded bras and our society that promotes this. Why are breasts so targeted? Why do men pay money to see women's breasts? Why did she take away a part of her that so many men and women seem to want? Should she tell him what people have said to her? Like, "Someday you will be angry for having the breast reduction." Or, from a counselor, "You need to take care that you don't present your decision as doing something to spite men or to keep them from looking at you and not taking you seriously." Why not, if that was the exact reason she did it?

Christy hated men looking at her breasts, at her that way. Yet she was obsessed with breasts. It was just about the first thing she saw on all women. Young, old, overweight, thin – it didn't matter; she looked at them all. It was not sexual. She was trying to find out what fascinated men about the female breast.

Christy often compared hers to theirs, speculating about what their breasts looked like when they were naked, how they'd sit without a bra, if they were real or fake. If they looked fake, Christy tried to figure out why they did it, what their lives were like for them to make that decision. She didn't understand how someone could mutilate her body, stick a foreign object under her skin and think it made her look better? Christy wondered why these great women in this great country couldn't love themselves the way they were.

And Christy always felt like a hypocrite because she had also gone under the knife. She tried to convince herself it was because she would one day suffer with back trouble, but that wasn't why she had done it.

In spite of this, she was thankful that she had had her breast reduction because it made her feel so much better about herself, physically and emotionally. Now men looked at her face, not her breasts like they used to. Maybe women were in two categories, the ones who want men to look at them like a sex object and the ones who want men to treat them with respect.

Christy thought breasts were interesting, but not nearly as beautiful or interesting as the women themselves. The way women walk, carry themselves, but especially their determination. That's what men should pay money to see: movies about women's lives and struggles. Christy once heard a man say that women should come with instruction manuals. If he took the time to listen or be interested in women's lives instead of their breasts, he would have his instruction manual.

Christy was eighteen when she had her breast reduction. Because she felt she had been on her own most of her life, she made this very important decision alone. She researched and analyzed it until the moment the decision was made.

Christy's breasts had become too large for the person she was. She enjoyed working out and was an active member of her local gym. She wanted to do aerobics, but her breasts were so heavy it was uncomfortable and embarrassing. A sports bra didn't help.

She was so discouraged, she quit.

She tried jogging but was too uncomfortable.

Christy tried wrapping ace bandages tightly around her chest, but it didn't work. Her breasts were too heavy. She gave herself a body-wrap with saran wrap, thinking it would sweat away the fat from her breasts and even tried to jog with it wrapped around her. It made her sweat and itch, but it didn't help.

She was self-conscious. She wore large, loose-fitting clothes and learned to slouch so she wouldn't look so large. She hated what her body had become.

The way she was treated by men was the worst of it all, not just high school boys, but grown men. They didn't look at her face when they spoke to her; they looked at her chest. Christy's breasts represented sex to them, and at her age, she wasn't ready to be a part of that world. She didn't date boys, go clothes shopping or hang out with friends for fear of somebody mentioning the size of her breasts.

At the gym, Christy changed to the stationary bike, envying the other women doing aerobics. They were wearing t-shirts in the summer while she wore over-sized sweatshirts, and men talked to their faces not their breasts.

The decision was made. At her first appointment, the doctor's assistant handed Christy a book of before and after shots of breast reductions. Christy was impressed and knew this was the answer. They talked about what would happen during surgery, about the scars under her breasts, up to and around her nipples that would fade in time. Most people would just assume she had lost weight, so it was up to her if she wanted to tell them differently. They also discussed how Christy's self-esteem would improve. One woman left her fiancé after being with him for three years, realizing after the operation that she deserved better. Another woman lost a lot of weight and started enjoying life more. She took up biking, dancing and especially dating. But all Christy could think about was how soon she could have it done, for her own reasons.

At the second appointment, the doctor, a middle-aged man with graying hair and a kind, yet serious, face examined her. As Christy sat there naked from the waist up, he commented on the marks on her breasts.

"What size bra do you wear?" he asked.

"Thirty-four C," Christy said.

"You are a D cup, your bra is too small."

Any other time, from any other person, that comment would have depressed Christy for a week, humiliating and embarrassing her. But now she knew her bra would be too big soon and she couldn't wait.

"What size do you want to be?" he asked.

Christy's high school friends had small breasts, and she was envious of them. She remembered sitting around a table in the cafeteria with about four of her closest friends. Vicki pulled the front of her shirt down low, exposing the upper part of her chest. She pushed her arms together against her breasts and said, "Look, cleavage," leaning into the center of the table. The others, laughing, joined in to show off their self-made cleavage. When Christy didn't join in, they started making comments about the size of her breasts.

Later, Christy told one of her best friends about how she thought she looked deformed. Searching for the right thing to say, her friend said that as long as she wore her hair long and full like she did, it wasn't noticeable. What else could she say?

"I want to be flat-chested. Would that be AA?" Christy asked.

He said the lowest he'd go was a B cup. Christy argued, but if B was all he'd give her, she would take it. When his assistant came to take the before shots of Christy's breasts, Christy was excited, she couldn't believe it — it was really going to happen.

Because Christy would eventually have problems with her back and shoulders, the insurance was approved. Christy was thrilled because it was the only way she could have afforded it.

"I don't want to wait. I'll take the appointment you have in four days," she said to Dr. Replog.

A few days later she was on her way to the hospital to have surgery. She would spend one night in the hospital, maybe two. Christy was excited, yet nervous. She remembered being concerned about the possibilities of having problems during surgery. She wondered if she needed a blood transfusion, would the blood be safe. Looking back, the worst part of the whole experience was the several attempts it took to insert the IV.

Christy was in her hospital gown, hooked up to an IV and ready for surgery. Dr. Replog drew lines on Christy's breasts with a purple marker where the incisions would be made and explained a little more about what would be happening during the operation. He left the room with a comforting smile saying, "See you in surgery." Christy was sedated shortly after.

Christy didn't remember much about the surgery, but she remembered waking up in the middle of the night and realizing her IV needle had come out. Blood was flowing faster and faster as if squirting out from her arm, so Christy started trying to put the needle back in to stop it. "Nurse! Nurse!" she yelled.

The nurse ran in and turned on the light. "No, Christy! Stop!" She pulled on her latex gloves. "It's OK. I got it." She took the needle from Christy and gently slid it into a vein in Christy's hand, taping it down securely. She started cleaning up Christy's arm and they both noticed the pool of blood and solution that had accumulated under her skin. The nurse told her it would be OK.

The thick bandages wrapped all around her chest reminded her of the saran wrap and ace bandages. Christy was so thankful she had the surgery. She knew her life would change.

Most people said, "Wow! You look great! Did you lose weight?" Nobody really knew and Christy didn't tell.

While lying topless in front of Paul, Christy wished she could love her breasts. She wanted to love them and touch them. She wanted to hold them and discover them. She wanted them to be important to her in a strong, independent, separate-from-men way. But she didn't know how to do that. And maybe that was why she felt sadness.

Christy had been angry with her breasts for as long as she could remember. Then one day she found a strange lump.

Christy knew what to expect with a mammogram. She'd seen pictures, heard the stories and watched Oprah. She also knew that she was young to have one.

Christy was prepared. She stood up to the machine strong and ready. It didn't hurt, but it was uncomfortable because of what they were looking for, having somebody touch her breasts in a non-sexual way, and then the machine flattening out her breasts, horizontally and vertically.

The nurse had her positioned perfectly. She told Christy to hold her breath so she could take the picture... Christy told her she wasn't doing well. Suddenly the machine released Christy's breast and the nurse guided her back to her chair. It wasn't until she was seated that she realized how weak she was. Ten seconds later Christy would have fainted. She was blacking out and sweating, shaking and weak. The nurse offered Christy juice. She accepted. Christy guzzled it down and told her she was ready to go again. She made Christy wait a bit longer.

Between each picture Christy had to sit down and rest so she wouldn't faint or throw up. After getting the mammogram, she was in the waiting room with other women, wearing their gowns over their naked breasts. They were either waiting their turn or waiting to be told they could get dressed and go home. The gowns didn't fit very well. All of the women were pulling and tucking to keep themselves covered.

Christy wanted to ask all these uncomfortable strangers to open their gowns, to not feel so uncomfortable. "We are all beautiful women and shouldn't feel so uncomfortable around each other. We should embrace each other." The others had at least twenty years on Christy, but she didn't care. She wanted them to talk; she wanted them to ask each other if this is a yearly checkup or to have somebody volunteer the information that they have cancer or that they had cancer and it may be back again. Or they are scared because they found a lump. Or it runs in the family so she had to be checked every six months. Or she's waiting for an ultrasound not a mammogram because her breasts are too dense.

Some of the women looked at her with pity, Christy thought, imagining she had a husband and some little children at home and may possibly have cancer. She wanted to tell them that she had a breast reduction and has scar tissue, so she is not sure if her lump is scar tissue from her breast reduction or something else. She would tell them that she didn't have a husband or children because she didn't know how to have a relationship. She would tell them that all she does is have sex with men and keep them at a distance. Maybe she would tell them how she sometimes fears she has HIV and has never been tested. And if it isn't HIV that gets her, maybe it will be cancer because she has not loved herself. How could she not have a disease after what she has put her body through? Would she tell them how she used to cut herself so she could feel something, or how the breast reduction helped her with her bulimia? Or what if the cutting of her breasts was the ultimate cutting something out of her, an imperfection. Would she tell them how she really just wanted her breasts removed?

And maybe the opening of the gown is not exposing breasts, but opening and exposing our hearts so we can support each other. Christy pictured that she would be the first to open hers. Would they be judgmental? Would they cause more disease with their disapproving energy, or would they support her and love her enough to fight the cancer off? Christy always believed it was our emotions that caused and conquered disease.

Christy was called back for more mammogram photos and then an ultrasound. Christy wasn't doing well. The lubricated ultrasound reminded her of the time she went to a massage therapist to work on some of her scar tissue to try to break it up. Christy didn't even know she needed help; her breasts were fine. But Christy had wanted to see what would happen and maybe the little bit of numbness would go away. Maybe Christy would be able to love her breasts. Maybe they needed to be touched in a non-sexual way to make them heal, to make Christy heal.

The massage therapist's office was in his house and his wife, who was a counselor, was home. Christy lay on the table trying to get comfortable when he came in. He tried to be careful about seeing her breasts, but Christy needed to show him. She sat up and exposed her breasts. "See," she said. "The scars go like this, underneath," She pulled her breast up to show him the scar, "up to the orialis and around it." She grabbed her left breast with her right hand and pulled it in toward her sternum. She pointed out the area where she had lost feeling. "I'm numb over here, just on this side. It's not that big a deal, but I just thought maybe this would be good for me." She lay back down and covered herself. "Whatever you think is fine with me, but I am a little uncomfortable with being touched where I have no feeling, and I'm nervous about a man massaging my breast."

"I understand. We will take it easy today. There is not a lot I can do until we establish trust, and we can't push that."

It helped that his wife was in the next room.

He started by rubbing the scar tissue from her armpit to the lower side of her left breast, never really touching what Christy considered her breast. Within minutes, Christy started to cry.

"Do you want me to stop?"

"I don't know."

He continued.

"It's OK to cry. Let it out."

She told him to stop.

He said he would step out of the room for a minute and give her some time.

When he came back in, he said, "I spoke with my wife, and she is willing to come in and be with you if you'd like."

"Yes," Christy said and cried even harder.

The massage continued along with pulling on her arm to stretch some of her muscles and tissue. Christy continued crying while his wife held her hand. He stopped the massage early and gave her some exercises to do at home. Though Christy thought it was healing for her, she never went back. She was embarrassed and didn't understand what happened, why she was so emotional. She didn't want to go through it again.

After Christy told Paul about her experience with the massage therapist, he encouraged her to find another one to finish what the first one started.

"We have so many great clinics here, I know you could find one where you feel comfortable. I'll go with you. I'll hold your hand."

"You'd laugh!"

"Christy."

"OK, fine. I'll go if you start taking your cocktail."

He dropped the subject.

8.

Talking with Paul stirred up all kinds of memories about her body, and later that night while Christy was getting ready for bed, she remembered a night she spent in a hotel while she was away on a modeling trip.

It would be a chance to get away and have some fun.

After she checked in, Christy quickly got into her swimsuit and went to the small indoor pool. She was alone. She swam laps until her arms and legs felt thick and heavy, then went to the sauna. The sauna was cold, so she turned it on and jumped back into the pool for another twenty laps.

Christy was glad she had the place to herself. She wanted time away from people for the night. The two-hour drive and her period on its way gave her a slight headache. Christy only got headaches for three reasons: lack of water, lack of caffeine or because her period was coming. She liked to be alone during that time of the month.

Christy pulled herself up on the ledge and out of the pool, dripping. She wondered if her triceps looked defined. She hurried to the sauna eager for the heat. She sat on the cedar bench. It was dingy and dark and suddenly her gratitude for being alone turned to fear. The small box of cedar made her feel trapped. All the carvings in the wood at first made her nervous then suddenly intrigued her. "B & S 4 ever" with a heart around it made her smile. But the lightly scratched "fat ass" and "BITCH" made her think of herself. She knew at times she was crabby, and she thought her ass was fat. Her bloating and water weight gain didn't help.

For the most part Christy was happy with her body. That was an odd thought coming from her, considering her past issues with her body. She had always considered herself a recovering bulimic, thinking about it almost every day and knowing that if she wasn't careful she could fall right back into trouble.

In high school, Christy started her dieting by fasting and only drinking grapefruit juice. But by the end of her three-day fast, she would binge and feel awful. The next time she'd try to fight the binge after the fast but always failed. Because of the failure, she lost even more self-esteem.

Her eating habits and body image became more important to her than anything else. It didn't take long, and she was making herself throw up after every eating binge. She had to throw up to get rid of the evidence that she was a failure. The evidence would show up on her hips and thighs and stomach that she was not strong enough to diet. She was not strong enough to be in charge of her body and be thin. She'd make a promise to herself, no more binging. Then she'd break the promise and binge. She hated that she wasn't stronger, that she didn't have more discipline. So she would stick her finger down her throat and get the food out of her, she'd get rid of it. It was like an apology, or making it up to herself by fixing the mistake of binging.

Christy started to lose weight. Maybe she had control of this after all. She became more obsessed with getting rid of the food than eating it to begin with. She found new ways to get it out of her. Not only did Christy throw up after everything she ate or drank, besides water, but she started abusing Ex-lax. Christy stole the boxes of pills or money to supply her addiction. She was up to about thirty Ex-lax a day, whether she ate anything or not and about ten diet pills a day to help curb her appetite.

By this time, it was noticeable something was going on. She had dropped twenty pounds and had burst blood vessels in and around her eyes. She made up stories about the blood in her eyes. Like she had the flu and kept dry heaving so her eyes turned that way. A teacher was worried, so she called an eye doctor and the game was up. The eye doctor told her Christy was probably bulimic. A few days before Christmas break, the teacher took Christy aside and asked her if she was bulimic. Christy denied it. But she knew the teacher was keeping a close eye on her, which infuriated Christy. She wanted to scream at her to mind her own fucking business!

The teacher had asked Christy to lick a stamp and put it on an envelope for her. Christy didn't want to, knowing the glue had calories, but felt she didn't have a choice with the teacher watching her. Christy was angry believing the teacher wanted her to be fat. She licked the stamp, then asked to use the restroom. That teacher followed her and heard her throwing up.

It was the day before Christmas break. She confronted Christy, "Did you just throw up?"

"No."

"Did you just throw up?"

"No."

"Did you just throw up?"

"Yes," Christy said and started crying.

She walked with Christy straight to the counselor's office. She got on the phone and told a doctor she had a student who admitted she was bulimic.

Christy wanted to scream, "I am not, you stupid bitch! I never said that!" Christy hated her for calling her that. The anger was overwhelming, and all she could do was cry.

Thinking back, Christy realized it was a cry of relief. The secret she was carrying around with her, the pain, wasn't only hers anymore. The hole that she had fallen into, somebody just threw down a rope for Christy to climb out. But she was only feeling fear and anger for having to come out of her secret place.

Christy grabbed her room key and carved an X across "fat ass" then carved "Teachers Rule" in one of the only clear spots left on the cedar. Carving made her think of cutting, another one of her many issues. She knew her cutting wasn't as extreme as others, but she knew she suffered from it.

Cutting was different from the bulimia. Being bulimic was such a private thing that she kept to herself. The cutting, sometimes she couldn't hide, or didn't want to. While she was bulimic, she was sent to the hospital two times from terrible stomach pain. Both times the doctor accused her of having a tubal pregnancy, even though Christy was still a virgin. It was fun for her to know something the doctor didn't. She also liked the way people looked at her when she had burst blood vessels in her eyes. It made her feel special. She even liked her scars from her breast reduction. They were marks of honor, important stuff.

In her sociology class in high school, Christy's teacher would give twenty extra points for anyone who could start a new fad. Christy didn't need the extra credit, but decided to pierce her hand anyway, just for fun. She took a needle and thread and sewed the flap of skin on her hand between her thumb and index finger. She got twenty extra points.

Later Christy started getting things pierced. She had her belly button pierced long before it was the in thing to do. She got a few small tattoos in places that were supposed to be the most painful but were still in places where nobody would know. Her clitoris ring was supposed to be her grand finale. She thought she would stop doing these painful things. She didn't stop. She started cutting imperfection out of her body. Every bump or mole or freckle or anything she thought was wrong with her was cut out or burned with acid. She liked the acid because the pain lasted longer.

Christy looked at her hands but they no longer had the scars from all the cuts she used to make in them. She used to take a sharp pair of scissors and grab skin and cut little pieces of her flesh off the back of her hands. She would stop only after her hands were full of blood. The blood didn't come right away. She could cut at least ten on her hand before she saw blood. Then she would do her other hand. For weeks after, she would wear oversized shirts that hung past her hands to keep them covered until they healed.

Christy looked again at her body before putting on her pajamas and felt very lucky to have lived this long and to be in a much better place with her life. She crawled into bed.

9.

Christy continued sneaking Paul's medication into his food whenever she had the chance. He wasn't improving from what she could tell, but she wasn't discouraged.

It was Saturday morning, almost noon. Christy and Paul were working on the book photos and waiting for Brian.

"How did you get me to do this Christy?" Paul asked.

"Do what?"

"Go on the boat," he said. "Brian's been trying to get me out there since the day we met."

"Easy. You'd do anything for me 'cause you love me," she teased.

Paul said, "I do... I do love you."

Christy's smile left her face, and she suddenly wanted to confess about his medication. Tears welled in her eyes. "I love you too, Paul."

Brian knocked, poked his head in and yelled, "You guys ready?"

Christy hollered back, "Oh, yeah! We're ready." She helped Paul up and they met Brian in the hall.

"Where's your stuff?" Brian asked.

"Right by the door," Paul said.

"You guys brought warm clothes right? Cause it might rain."

"Yeah, we got it all," Christy said.

"Great. Let's go!" Brian was full of energy and obviously excited to have Christy and Paul on his boat. "Remember, this whole weekend is on me." He picked up both bags by the door. Christy helped Paul and they headed out the door. She purposely left the cameras at home.

Paul sat in the back seat of the big, green, older SUV that Brian drove. Brian had to run a couple of errands before they went to the boat. They stopped at the grocery store to pick up food for dinner, snacks and ice. Brian also picked up a deck of cards in case it rained and they were stuck inside. They stopped at a gas station and then were on their way to the boat.

The boat was beautiful and huge, white with a blue stripe.

They carried everything to the boat and set it on the dock. With Brian's help, Paul stepped inside. Brian handed him what they carried. The heavy stuff they left on the dock and went back for more. They carried the last load over and Christy climbed onto the boat. Brian handed her the heavy tools and ice while Paul put the groceries away.

"Well, show us your boat," Christy demanded.

"Oh, I'm sorry. Well, this is the kitchen or galley, living room area or salon. Over here," he walked to the front, "the bow, is the front bedroom or stateroom and front bathroom or head. This back here, aft, would be the master bedroom with its own bath.

"Or head." Christy said. "Yes, this boat is definitely male."

Brian grinned. "Male boat, huh?" he nodded his head. "OK then." He pointed and walked into the master bedroom. "This is where you guys will be tonight if you don't mind sharing a bedroom."

"That's fine with me," Christy said. Both bedrooms had two single beds.

"The closet is there if you want to hang up anything."

"Yeah, Brian. I'd like to hang my sweats up."

Brian wasn't used to Paul joking and started pulling out a hanger for him. When Christy started laughing, Brian turned around. "What?" When he noticed Paul grinning too, he understood.

"Brian, we don't need to hang anything or iron anything; we're here to hang loose and have fun!"

Brian poked Christy in the ribs and called her a smart aleck.

It was clear Paul was happy to be there. "Are we going to sit at the dock all day? Let's get boating!" he said.

Brian's enthusiasm picked up again. "I have a few things to do. Christy, I'll need your help."

"OK." She followed him.

"No." He changed his mind wanting Paul to feel useful. "Paul can do it. Paul, could you come up here?"

Paul was happy to help or at least to be asked. "Sure."

"OK, first we need to take this down," he said pointing to the blue canvas covering the upper deck. "I'll hold it while you unzip. Why don't you start here?"

Paul stepped forward and started unzipping.

Christy watched from below. She was happy she got Paul to come out on the boat. She was also happy to be there. "I want to do something. What can I do?" she hollered up to them.

"And, this has nothing to do with you being a woman, but why don't you vacuum." He turned to Paul and started laughing.

When Paul started laughing too, Christy joined in. "Oh, all right! Where's the vacuum?" She pretended she was upset.

"It's in the front bedroom, behind the door," Brian told her. Paul and Brian smiled.

The vacuuming was done. Paul and Brian together cleaned off the deck. Christy even volunteered to dust, but Brian told her the work was done and it was now time to play.

Christy followed him to the upper deck. Brian started the boat, then hopped off the boat and pulled all the ropes. He hopped back on board and sat at command. He asked Christy to stand on the side of the boat and push on the tall pilings to keep the boat from rubbing against the dock while Brian backed it out. Paul sat next to Brian and watched them both.

Brian backed the boat out, and they were on their way. Christy came back and sat on the other side of Brian.

"Are you guys warm enough?" Brian asked.

"Yeah, I am," Christy answered. "Are you Paul?"

"Yes, I'm fine."

"It's windy, but a beautiful day," Christy said. The splashes of the water against the boat were soothing, along with the rocking it caused. There were a few boats out and past them were the trees, a beautiful variety of palms, and huge homes.

"In a while we'll pull off into an area port where the trees will block us from the wind. I know just the spot. Then we can make the burgers and watch the sun set. The sun should be warm on us."

"Sunset... why, what time is it?"

"It's about 4:00. The sun starts to set around 6:00. And we won't make it out to the ocean today. It's pretty rough and it's getting late. We'll just stay inner coastal tonight and see how tomorrow is."

"Wow. Winter is right around the corner," Paul said. "It seems like just yesterday it set at 9:00."

"Yep, even in Florida."

After a great tour through the waterways, and seeing the celebrities' homes, Brian docked the boat on an island beach away from everyone. Christy and Brian drank beer and danced around while Paul made the burgers on the grill at the back of the boat. The music was loud and the breeze was light. Dusk was moving in, the pinks and oranges were fading.

Christy loved where she was and who she was with. Her beer was beginning to affect her so when Brian was in front of her dancing around, she yelled, "Paul!" and yanked Brian's black shorts down to his ankles.

Brian acted as if he hardly noticed. He casually pulled them back up and kept dancing.

Paul and Christy laughed. "I'd go for it if I were you," Paul teased.

"Really? Cool!" Christy reached over and pulled them down again.

Again Brian hardly reacted. When he bent over to pull them up, Christy swatted his bare ass, this time making Brian turn quickly in Christy's direction. But Christy was already down the stairs and into the cooler reaching for another beer.

Brian ducked down to see her. "Maybe you should wait until after your burger."

"Or maybe I should drink it with my burger," Christy sassed back.

"Let her be. She's fine. Let her have some fun," Paul yelled from the back of the boat.

"OK, Paul, but she's your responsibility."

"And I'm yours. Then that makes you Christy's responsibility," Paul teased.

Christy heard and stood on the stairs. "That's right! So Brian get down here and do me!"

Brian pointed to Christy, raised his eyebrows, and gave a questioning look to Paul.

Paul was laughing at Christy. He shrugged his shoulders and said, "I don't know what to tell you... But the burgers are done. Grab your plates."

Christy hopped downstairs and grabbed the plates for all three. Brian took the opportunity to try to get her back. "I'm glad you don't have to be told what your responsibilities are as a woman... Waiting on men."

Christy turned around and threw one of the blue plastic plates like a frisbee back into the kitchen. "There you go!" She said and walked over to Paul with the two plates.

Brian couldn't help but laugh knowing he got a rise out of her. He walked down and got his plate.

Paul scooped up Christy's burger and said, "I sense some chemistry in the air."

Christy smiled. "Why, you got the hots for Brian?" She winked and turned to walk back to the kitchen almost running into Brian.

"I got your bun for you Christy," Brian said. "Being a woman you should have known to grab the buns while you were down there."

"Yeah well, you got the only buns I want," Christy teased. "Who wants ketchup? I'll get it."

"No!" Brian said. "Not on Paul's burgers. He seasons them too good to ruin them with ketchup."

"OK." She sat and started eating.

When they were finished eating and cleaning up, Christy and Paul went to their bedroom to put more clothes on to keep warm. The fall chill was moving in, though Christy didn't notice much because of the alcohol. It was Paul and Brian who wanted her to also add a sweatshirt and a pair of socks. Christy sat on the bed while Paul grabbed the thick, tan, wool socks and each of Christy's feet to put them on her.

"You're such a good person, Paul," Christy said.

"Now don't get all sappy on me... give you a little beer and you turn to mush," Paul teased. "You're a good person, too, Christy. I'm glad you came into my life."

He was done putting her socks on her, so she grabbed his grey socks from him and did the same for him.

Brian yelled down, "You guys listen, this is my favorite song!"

Paul and Christy both knew it. It was Tori Amos singing "God."

"That's odd, isn't it?" Paul asked Christy. "Different from his whole women attitude from earlier."

"Yeah," Christy agreed.

"You know, he's really a good guy and giving you a hard time is probably because he likes you."

Christy showed interest. "He's single?"

"Yes."

"Well, I don't have time for a boyfriend. I don't even want one. It never works out; it's better to stay friends."

"Christy, I'm not talking marriage. I'm just saying that you're both good people, and I'd hate to see you so guarded that you won't give a good guy a chance."

"Paul, you really don't know about me. My life hasn't been easy and maybe I just don't want to make it any more difficult. I'm happy right now being alone with a good friend... You. That's all I want and it's all I'm capable of right now."

"Christy, my life hasn't been easy either, but I'll tell you one thing... When I opened myself up to allow love in, that is when I really began to live..." He paused and looked down. "I loved him. And I killed him." He started crying. "I miss him."

"How do you know who had it?"

Paul's crying slowed. "After being together for about a year we went in together to get checked. I had it, he didn't. We used protection always after that. Every month he went in and got tested. Two months later he was HIV positive. Just under two years later he started getting sick. I remember when he found out. He came home and wasn't even mad. Before he died, he told me he hoped I'd have an easy journey and that he'd be waiting for me on the other side. I want to be with him again. We were meant to be. I love him."

Christy sat next to him on the bed and held him. She was torn about the medication.

"What's taking so long, guys," Brian yelled down before he saw. "Oops." He stopped.

"I'm sorry," Paul said. "The plan was to have a fun night."

"No, Paul, don't apologize. Are you OK?"

"Yes, I'm fine. I guess maybe I'm feeling guilty because I am having a good time and maybe I feel like I don't deserve it."

"Paul, you haven't done anything wrong," Christy said.

"You do deserve to be happy," Brian added. "And wouldn't he want you to be happy and enjoy the rest of your life?"

"Yes, he would." Paul started to smile. "He would want that."

"OK then," he said looking at them. "You two get yourselves together and join me on deck. I'm going to put on a nice slow song, and you get the first dance of this starry night. It isn't going to rain." He ran upstairs. "And, Christy," he yelled, "I get the second."

Paul stood and reached for Christy's hand. "Ready?"

"Yes." She stood and held his hand as they walked upstairs. The song playing was, "You've Got A Friend" by James Taylor. They walked straight over to the open area of the boat and began to dance. Christy could feel the warmth of his body, his life, pressed against hers. She didn't want to get emotional, but she couldn't help it. He had become her best friend and he would die soon. Plus her guilt of lying to him about his medication was tugging at her. Just when Christy was about to tell him the truth, a leaf blew down between them. It landed on Christy's sweatshirt close to her heart. Before she had a chance to reach for it, Paul picked it up, put it to his mouth and kissed it. Christy was so moved she took it from him and ran downstairs. She opened up the flat side pocket of her bag and stuck the leaf in. She quickly ran back up to finish her dance with Paul, but Paul was already sitting.

"Oh, no. It's my turn," Brian said pulling her away from Paul. Brian held her close. His large body was so different from Paul's. She liked it. She liked him.

It was a great night. They danced around on the boat. Later they talked and played cards, and when they all three had to go pee, Christy stood between them and with her fingers she pulled up on her vulva and pissed off the boat with them. She liked how the stream falling looked just like theirs.

Paul was tired so they all decided to go to bed. Christy could tell Brian wanted her to stay up with him, but she didn't want to get into an uncomfortable situation. Christy could jump into bed with him, but she wanted to make love with someone. She wanted to like where she was so much that love would come naturally. She didn't want to have sex. She wanted to make love because she never had.

That night Christy tossed and turned and kept having dreams about Brian. Some sexual dreams and others were about them being married and having children and a Pug named Shorty.

Between dreams, Christy thought about Brian, about his body against hers as they danced. He was strong. He was sexy. She wished she hadn't danced with him. She rolled over and tried to go back to sleep. What did she know about him? He's a nurse. He cares about Paul. He's good looking. He likes boating. He likes sports, especially Miami Heat and Miami Dolphins. He works out. He drives an old, green SUV. He likes Tori Amos. She was tired and that was all she could come up with. She wasn't sure if she wanted to learn more.

The next morning Paul was the first one up. Christy and Brian woke to the smell of breakfast cooking.

Christy went into the kitchen. "It smells great."

"Do you want some coffee?" Paul asked.

"Sure."

"I'll get it," Brian said coming out of the other bathroom. Christy stayed seated and smiled to herself because Brian was waiting on her.

"You must be feeling pretty good," Brian said to Paul while he poured the coffee.

"Yes, I'm feeling better than I have in a long time." He turned from the stove. "Thank you, Christy, for getting me out here. And thank you, Brian, for asking again."

"You're welcome. Thank you for coming, and thank you for changing your mind about taking the medication."

Heat shot through Christy and panic filled her.

"What? What are you talking about? I haven't changed my mind."

Christy wasn't ready for this and was unable to get a word out.

"Yes. I brought your medication over to you last week."

"Not to me!"

"To Christy... She said you changed your mind."

They both turned and looked at her. "I'm sorry! I'm sorry!" she cried. "I don't want you to die! I don't want you to die!" She got up, ran to the back bathroom and locked the door.

She couldn't stop crying. She was loud and didn't care what they thought. Christy had never loved or been loved like she had with Paul, and she didn't want to lose it, lose him.

10.

Christy walked into Paul's bedroom. Brian was telling Paul to make a fist. Paul was weak.

"Paul..." Brian paused. "Paul, we're going to have to start searching for veins in your feet."

"I figured," Paul said in his weak voice.

Christy began to cry.

"I think we need to get another nurse for you, too."

"My veins are closing up, aren't they?"

"Yes," Brian said, "They are, but we have some alternatives."

Paul's eyes were circled in dark. His skin was graying. He had shortness of breath and was barely able to cough. Paul's vision was fading in his right eye.

"We could try a blood transfusion," Brian suggested.

"No!" Paul snapped.

Christy couldn't stand there another second. She turned to leave and slammed the door behind her, intending Paul to hear and know that she had heard him say no. Why did he want to leave her?

Christy was aching like she'd never ached before. She wanted to scream and crawl out of herself, out of the pain. But she couldn't. She didn't know how to make it stop. She didn't know how she could live without him.

After a few minutes, Brian came out after Christy. She was in Paul's office looking at the boxes of personal things that he had been packing on good days. The boxes were marked with big blue numbers. Christy wasn't sure what the numbers meant. She assumed each number was a person, family or charity the box was to go to.

"Christy."

"What?"

"We tried… This is what he wanted."

"I know, but I'm pissed!" She began crying.

Brian sat down next to her on the couch and he held her and let her cry. He pushed her hair away from her face with his fingertips and kept gently caressing the back of her head.

Her sadness turned to fear. She could feel Brian's tenderness and caring and love, and she didn't want to.

She pulled away from him, rubbed her eyes and took a deep breath to calm herself.

"Did he know I was standing there?"

"Yes, he saw you."

"He saw me?"

"Yes, he saw you. Then you slammed the door…" Brian continued, "Christy, he loves you. He's worried about you."

"Yeah, yeah. I know. Poor little Christy, never loved, always let down. Everybody has to worry about poor Christy… "

"Really? That's not what I see. I'm not worried about you at all. You're talented. You're smart. You're strong."

She stared at him. She'd rather be pitied. It's easier. She didn't want someone to think she was strong. She wanted everybody to feel so sorry for her that they — Paul — would decide to get the transfusion. She'd rather they think that if Paul died, she'd die and maybe then somebody would step in and make Paul live.

Brian looked at his watch. "I'm going to go check on him."

"OK. Are you staying tonight?"

"Yes, I'm staying until he has someone else here nights. It won't be long now, Christy. But you already knew that."

Her eyes welled up again. "Let's do the transfusion! I heard you say we could do a transfusion. Let's do that!"

"He said no, Christy. You better start making peace with this."

Christy nodded, trying to fight the tears and headed upstairs.

She took off her clothes and stood in front of the mirror. She had lost weight. Her ribs, hipbones and collarbones made the rest of her appear caved in. Her face had sunk, making the lines in her face that she hated stand out even more. She wondered if she had AIDS or if it was stress. She didn't care; either way she was in trouble.

She hated taking showers. She hated doing anything with her hair and makeup, but she managed to keep up with the showers and pulled her hair back into a ponytail. She only did it for Paul, to be clean around him.

She turned on the shower and began to cry. She stepped into the hot water. The hot water made her skin tingle and turn red, but it felt good. She hoped it would wash away her tension. She was so afraid to be without Paul. He was the only man she'd ever loved.

11.

Before she met Paul, Christy had been modeling at an art school three days a week after work. It was supposed to be temporary, but she had been helping out the instructor for almost a year. He was the first person she had ever modeled for, just over five years earlier.

She was a nude model and she was sick of it. She would soon be twenty-eight years old, and she'd done nothing to better her life. She wanted to be the artist, not the model. But at the time she figured she'd learn from the other artists; she didn't have the money to go to school.

In the beginning, during her younger rebellious years, "I'm a nude model" created a great pick-up line at the bars. Her target never believed it, but she enjoyed his looking her body up and down, picturing it. And she loved the clarity of his knowing what she wanted that night, to show him her body and to see his.

At first, Christy did enjoy her modeling, and she knew she was good at it. She learned a lot: lighting, paint types, great deals, where to shop for what you need, what to try next, charcoal, oil or watercolors, canvas or recycled paper, who to talk to, where to put your art when finished, what gallery, who charges what. On her days off, she was invited to sit in and do her own work, no charge, which she did often. She believed this was all helping her get closer to her goal of being an artist and that she was making contacts along the way.

Though she had only modeled for this school for a few months, she knew the routine. She quickly became the model in demand. She modeled for many different artists in their home studios, some world famous. Her image hangs in galleries, is a statue in a park in New York, a huge bronze sculpture in Chicago at a college and has even made it to other countries, places she'd only dreamed about going.

In some ways, it was an ego trip for her. She knew she was the favorite model. The instructor, Craig, told her the artists often called to see who would be modeling. If he told them Christy, he knew they would be there. It was an adult class at this school, and they all had a spot in the local gallery.

Christy used to love walking through the gallery and seeing herself hanging on the walls, naked, for everyone to look at. She couldn't remember why she loved it. She used to tell people it was because when she died, she could continue on in some way, be immortal. Maybe a different form of having children.

With sad memories threatening to overwhelm her, Christy quickly undressed and walked out of the changing room in her white robe. She sat down on her stage and waited for the artists to adjust their easels. The smell of turpentine was especially strong that day. She had been in the same place so many times it didn't matter to her who was there, who was late, or who wouldn't show at all. She liked most of the artists, and they all liked her.

Christy was beautiful. One of her best features was her long wavy, sometimes curly, depending on the weather, brownish blond hair. Her face, as one man told her, had untraditional beauty. It was her wider nose that gave her so much character, and she liked it. But it was her body that most of the artists were impressed with and not in a sexual way. Christy had a talent for sculpting her body. She lifted weights and worked out in ways that would keep her body the way she wanted it, though she knew age and gravity were catching up to her.

After noticing a couple artists had added her breast reduction scars to their work, Christy became angry. So she started each class that had new artists by lifting her breasts and saying, "These are scars! I had a breast reduction when I was eighteen. Don't add them to your sketches and paintings."

She had never been ashamed of her body unless someone tried to turn it in to something dirty, or as she modeled, someone tried to turn her into something sexual. At the bar it was fine, expected and she was in control. But a student making a sexual comment meant the student was kicked out and no longer allowed in any of the classes Christy modeled for.

The last few artists came in and chose their places. It was time to adjust the lighting. Christy stood, let her robe drop to the hardwood floor and stepped onto the platform. She brushed her hair back off her shoulders and looked out to the audience. She always enjoyed their faces of confusion. She was no longer a naked body; she was now a problem for them to solve.

"Let's put the spot low and see how that looks," one man said.

The two men standing by adjusted the light.

"What do you think?" the instructor asked.

"No. I think it needs to be higher," a woman said.

One of the guys moved it up. "How's that?"

"Let's turn off the front ceiling lights and see how that looks."

A woman walked over and flipped the switch. Christy watched as they stared at her, but they weren't looking at *her*. They didn't even see her standing there, naked. She was not even a human being to them. Christy fought the tears and lost. She bent over, picked up her robe, not taking the time to put it on, and walked naked back to the dressing room. She sat on the stool, crying, trying to decide what to do. She could use the money. She didn't want these people to be angry at her because she wanted to work *with* them not *for* them. She wanted to attend the Stuttley School of Art, not model for them. She rocked back and forth trying to calm herself, trying to decide what to do.

There was a knock at the door. "Christy? Are you OK?"

"Craig, you can come in," she said and sniffed.

Craig was as big around as he was tall, and he barely fit as he stepped inside the dressing room. Christy was still sitting naked, not realizing it until he picked up her robe and handed it to her. She covered herself.

"Craig, you've known me for a long time, and you know my goal. I want to be on the other side. I don't want to be the model anymore. I want to be the artist. And it's hitting me today... right now. I can't do this anymore," she said wiping her eyes.

He looked disappointed. "Well, Christy, we really need you tonight. These people are depending on you."

"Oh, come on. Don't put that guilt on me. It's an art class. The world won't fall apart if I'm not modeling tonight. Besides, you have a naked body under those clothes. Why don't you model if it's so important that they have one?"

He lowered his head. "All right, Christy, I knew this day was coming. Here you go." He reached into his shirt pocket and paid her what she would have made that night.

"Why are you paying me? I'm not working tonight."

"I know, but you've helped me out more times than one. You deserve it."

"OK, now you're really making me feel guilty," Christy giggled through her tears.

"I'm not meaning to," he said. "Wait here a minute. I have something for you." He turned and left the room.

Christy quickly got dressed and stepped outside the dressing room just as Craig was approaching. He handed her a piece of paper. "Christy, I know you like art but you never fail to mention photography when we talk. This is a guy I know who... Well, I mentioned you and he's willing to meet with you."

"Who is he?" she asked, unfolding the paper Craig had given her.

"A friend of mine."

Christy was shocked. "I know him... I know his work! He's famous!" she exclaimed. "He's your friend?"

"Yes! I have friends," he said smiling.

"Thank you," she said and gave him a hug.

"Why don't you get out of here, I have some modeling to do." He smiled to her. "Give him a call tonight!"

"You're modeling? Then I'm staying!" She joked. She gave him another hug and took off out the door.

Christy couldn't believe how much her life had changed from that day, and she knew Craig initiated that change. She wanted to call and thank him.

12.

Paul and Christy sat in the living room talking about his future and plans for his death. Paul was now in a wheelchair and had a full-time nurse and full-time help from Brian.

Christy was often alone with Paul to talk about his wishes for the book and to continue taking photos. Much of the book was complete, and it was up to Christy to finish it. Knowing Paul was close to death was hard on her, but it was during these times she felt closer than ever to him. She could see that he was at peace with himself. And it was rubbing off on her. After all of the time watching Paul and working on the book, she was considering getting tested. She wanted to know her fate, and she felt she was prepared for anything. She finally told Paul the truth about her own fear that she too may have contracted the virus. She openly talked about her own carelessness with sex and the many men she went through. Christy talked about how she didn't want to be with anyone else until she knew; that's why she avoided Brian. She didn't want to be responsible for somebody else's life. She hadn't even been responsible with her own.

"What about you? What about your future, your life?" he asked. "What about your dreams? You need to get tested. Christy, what if you don't have it? Have you thought about that?"

"Well, that's why even when I find out and if I don't have it, I still don't want to be with anyone unless it's forever and committed, or I'll just be committed to myself..."

"That's the key. First you must be committed to yourself," Paul interrupted.

"I know, but isn't the word 'committed' unfriendly? Who really wants to be committed? It sounds like you're being taken away to a mental institute," Christy laughed.

"Did you know that not too long ago educated women were thought to have lost their appeal?"

"Where did that come from?"

"I just remembered reading it... and looking at you, I have a really hard time understanding it. I've learned so much about you in such a short time. I think you are incredible. You're smart and tough, more so than you give yourself credit for. When I look at you, I see nothing but beauty. I'm glad I wasn't alive then."

"Maybe you were. And that's why you came back gay. We're all too smart for you, too smart to be attractive," Christy teased.

Paul smiled then gave a little laugh. "No. I'm only attracted to educated people, male or female. That's why I was immediately attracted to you."

"Are you hitting on me?"

"Is it working?"

"Of course."

"So you believe in that, Christy, reincarnation?"

"Yes, I do."

"Why?"

"Well, for all kinds of reasons. Mainly because I really haven't a clue what happens to us. So there's no reason for me not to believe. But one thing I question is that when we die our body cools and the only thing that has left is our spirit. Our heart is still there, our blood, brain, bones. Just our spirit leaving cools our body."

"Did I, a minute ago, say something about you being intelligent? Well, I take it back," Paul teased.

"I know. I know, but it's what I choose to believe."

"I'm kidding, Christy. I like it."

"I'm not one who is sure about anything, but I know there must be a strong connection between women and the earth, stronger than the connection with men. I know that women are on a twenty-eight-day cycle and so is the moon and so is the tide. I look at the beautiful moon, and I love being a woman. I look at the ocean, and I love being a woman. I'm learning to love my cycles, my emotions. I used to run from the emotional part of me and other women. I was afraid of it and thought it made me weak. I wanted to be more like a man.

"I wouldn't cry at sad movies. I wouldn't cry if my feelings were hurt. I didn't let myself get too attached to anybody, especially men. I had sex with men the way I thought men had sex with women, no feelings, no commitment. I had many one-night stands; in fact, that's all they were. I didn't want anything else. But why would I? I didn't know anything else was possible.

Until a stupid one-night stand changed everything. I could kill that guy. Everything was just fine until he came along."

"Maybe you are a man," Paul chuckled.

"Maybe I am. What women do makes me not want to be a woman. Society makes it look like all women like to shop. I don't."

"Love it."

"All women cook. I don't."

"I love to cook."

"Women are supposed to clean and keep the house tidy."

"Love it," Paul said. "Well, it's clear you're not a gay man."

"Women are emotional and cry all the time… I can't say anything about that, I think in the last couple of years I've cried more than anyone. Making up for lost time, I guess."

"You're not a man, Christy. You're a woman. Get used to it."

"What about how in movies they make women look so stupid when they are having a baby… or why are women so irresponsible with their pads and tampons in public restrooms, it makes me sick."

"I don't know anything about that."

"Too many women cater to men and it ruins men. If the day comes when you're tired of being submissive and you want your way just once, they will find someone else because they know they can find someone to cater to them," Christy continued. "I know that sounds harsh, but what about all those negligees at all the stores? Especially during the holidays: Santa nighties and Valentine's Day teddies. If women were buying this stuff for themselves and they were single I'd say awesome. But buying it for some guy, I say yuck!"

"Christy, you might not be a woman either. Who are you? Where did you come from?"

"Ha! Ha!" Christy said in sarcasm. "I'm a woman, trying to be the best woman I can be while staying true to myself. I really shouldn't generalize so much, I'm sure there are some really great women out there. I'd love to find some great friends."

"Christy, you are not defined by being a man or a woman. You are who you are, and I think you're pretty cool."

"You are so nice to me." She stood and gave him a kiss on his head. "We got off subject. Now look at everything. Everything is made up of circles constantly moving, turning, the earth, the sun and moon. And the circle is constant, never ending."

"Like the wedding ring."

"Yeah, right," Christy said laughing. "But look at our water. All the water we have is all the water we'll ever have. It's in the lakes and oceans. It evaporates and rises then comes back down again in snow and rain. The snow melts and seeps into our earth for growth, to help the food chain around another circle, then runs off into the rivers to continue back to the oceans and again back to our sky. And we drink it, it goes through our bodies, is cleaned and reused. Have you ever drunk a glass of water while peeing? It's an odd feeling. Which brings us to recycling and how everything is and can be recycled in time. Why not our spirits, too?" Christy asked.

"World population is growing every year. Where are all the spirits coming from?"

"Well, maybe from extinct animals and split spirits."

"Split spirits?"

"Yes. Maybe we're splitting ourselves so everybody can have one. Maybe those are the rapists, murderers, child molesters and thieves. They are all the incomplete spirits," Christy continued. "So if people would stop having so many kids, we could start using our prisons as recycling centers or have less crowded schools. Plus, if we didn't have so many people, we wouldn't have so much garbage and pollution."

"Except the population rise is not from us having too many kids; it's because we are all living longer," Paul added. "And maybe we have so many murders, suicides and diseases because the spirits are needed to fill the incoming babies."

"Good point! One other thing, which I know sounds crazy, but what would happen if all little boys were fixed at birth? Then when they're older and have the money to pay for surgery to reverse it, that's when they have children. They have to want children and want to take good care of them. There would be no more trapping each other into a family or marriage because of an accidental pregnancy. There wouldn't be abortions. The only people who would have children would be the people who truly want them. Wouldn't our world be a better place?"

Paul's eyebrows raised, "Wow! Well, that just opens a whole other can of worms. You just took away everybody's freedom and made poor people unable to have children. Not to mention an increase in STDs."

"No, I didn't. I just eliminated the low income bracket all together. That's just it, everybody would be able to have children! Everybody who wanted them!"

"I see what you're saying. That's pretty deep. You could take that one a long way… how would that affect everybody…"

"…can really get the mind going thinking about stuff like that. I don't know, Paul. What are your thoughts? How do you feel about death?" Christy asked.

"Well, I've found peace in just relaxing and letting whatever happens happen. I'm not disbelieving the Bible stuff or the whole God thing, just in case." He winked at Christy.

"That's cute."

"Yeah, I know," he said. "My time is coming, Christy."

"Do you know when?"

"It won't be long."

Christy began crying. She moved to the floor at his feet and started holding his legs. She buried her head in his lap. "Paul." She sat silently touching him rubbing his legs, smelling his scent and feeling his heat. She could touch him, she could feel him. The love was touchable; he was touchable. She didn't want to lose it, him, ever. She wanted to hold him, hang on to him, keep him from leaving her. "What am I going to do without you?" she cried.

"Yes, Christy, what are you going to do when I'm gone? You should start making plans."

"I don't know, I'll worry about it later… Why wouldn't you take your medication? Why didn't you fight for your life? I've talked to Brian about the medication and how you felt on the boat, you felt good. Happy. Brian said the pills couldn't have worked that quickly. It was a state of mind you had that night, then you quit." Christy was sobbing.

"Christy, I didn't ask for this, but I got it and I want to do something positive, something good before I go, something unselfish. I've spent too much of my life being selfish. I have a mission and it is time to give, and I am, with your help," he said. "I would love to continue on. Having you around has probably prolonged everything anyway. But I had to finish what I started. I made the decision before you entered my life. That's why you entered my life in the first place because of all this, so isn't that a gift all on its own? Christy, I'm happy with my decision. I'm happy with the work you've been doing, we've been doing, on this book. I hope it will help."

"It will. But, Paul..."

"Please don't, Christy," he stopped her. "I'm tired. Will you help me back to bed?"

Christy got up and wheeled him back to the bedroom.

"Christy, if I don't wake up, remember, I love you." He coughed.

"What do you want for dinner?" She ignored what he said as if not giving him the choice.

"The peas and carrots and chicken."

"OK, I'll see you in a few hours," she ordered then turned to leave the room. "Oh, and Paul, I love you, too." She went to the kitchen to set out his jars of baby food.

13.

Christy lay in bed with Paul as she had many nights before. He was in good spirits. He was alert and seemed more like the Paul she met months ago. Paul was no longer hooked up to any medical equipment.

They lay on their sides facing each other. They held hands and listened to the thunderstorm.

A loud thunder rumble opened Christy's eyes wide with surprise, which made Paul laugh.

"It's OK," he said and squeezed Christy's hand.

"That was a big one!" she smiled.

The rain started pouring down. That sound was comforting after the thunder and lightning.

Paul rubbed Christy's hand with his thumb.

Christy leaned forward and gave Paul a tender gentle kiss on his dry lips. She slid the rest of her body closer to his, and rolled to her back. He snuggled in to her and lay his head on her chest.

"It's a perfect night." Paul said.

"Yes, it is. The night is singing to us."

He snuggled in trying to get even closer. He held on tight and so did she. They drifted off.

When Christy woke it was still raining and Paul was cool. She knew his spirit had left his body.

Christy lay there holding Paul's lifeless body. He was still holding onto her, his head firmly on her breast. She kissed his forehead. They lay there together, listening to the rain.

Christy was numb.

She was happy she had been with him when he took his last breath. She knew he was happy she was there, too. She could feel that his pain was gone, and he seemed to be at peace.

About an hour later, Christy eased her way out of bed and went for the camera and tripod. She set the camera up and lay back down next to Paul. She snapped several shots of the two of them, as she was crying. He was gone. Her best friend was dead.

She didn't plan to take photos of herself, but what about the people who are left behind, alone? Shouldn't people see *that* pain?

She took more pictures of Paul alone. Then she went to wake Brian in the spare bedroom.

Christy walked into Brian's room. She stood for a moment feeling uncomfortable being in his room seeing him vulnerable. It was dark, but there was light coming from the window; she could see where he was lying on the bed. She quietly stepped to him and touched his shoulder.

"Brian," she said, slightly shaking him. "Brian, wake up."

"What's wrong?" He sat up quickly.

"He's gone. Paul's gone."

"Well, did you check the bathr…" He stopped. "He's gone?"

"Yes. I don't know what I'm supposed to do now. Will you help me?"

Brian could tell Christy was in shock. He walked down the hall to Paul's room with Christy following. When they walked in, Christy started crying again.

Paul was lying there, cold and alone.

Christy was standing there, cold and alone.

She would never hear his voice again. She would never hear him cough. She would never see that look in his eyes again, the one of disappointment nor the one of love. She would never be told how to take the shot or how to adjust the lighting. She would never feel his warmth again, never hold him again. He would never hold her.

Brian felt Paul's forehead and checked for a pulse in his neck. Christy stood in the doorway and cried.

"Christy, do you have everything you need here?"

Christy realized what he was asking. "Yes, I think so."

"Come on, Christy. Stay strong for Paul."

"I am!" she hollered and held the camera back up as Brian pulled the sheet to cover him. "No! Wait!"

He stopped.

She stood there with the lowered camera and cried. "What am I going to do? What am I going to do?" She moaned in pain.

14.

At the funeral, Christy took pictures of Paul in the casket. He looked peaceful and almost happy. Paul had a lot of friends and many admirers of his work. It struck Christy as odd that so many people were there when he had always seemed so alone, like he had no one. She wondered if they stayed away because of their fear of AIDS or if Paul pushed them away because of it.

He was dressed in a tan, button-down shirt over a white t-shirt from an AIDS benefit he and Jim had been a part of before he got really sick. They were the clothes he'd picked out. He was so relaxed, but as much as Christy wanted to be happy for him, she couldn't. She missed him. She was mad at him for leaving her.

She cried as she continued shooting during the closing of the casket while people placed flowers on it, and even when he was being lowered into the ground. It was over. Paul was gone and the book was almost finished. She had only a few photos to add to the book before it went to press.

Christy had to pack and move. She found a place to live with Brian's help, a small studio in downtown Miami. Paul had told her she could take a few things from the house and all the photo equipment. Whatever she wanted. The rest was being auctioned off, along with the house, for AIDS research. His attorney was handling all of that. She did take her favorite poster from his office wall, a black and white photo of a nude man and woman squatting down intertwined. The woman had pale skin with dark hair, the man tanned skin with blond hair. Christy had always loved it. Even before she met Paul she remembered seeing it in magazines as an ad for cologne.

Christy sat on Paul's front step with a cup of coffee. She had cried so much in the last few weeks that she couldn't cry anymore. She tried to relax, meditate, but she couldn't. She was on the verge of deep depression and she knew it. She lay back on the cool cement, listening to the birds chirping. She knew it was spring, but she missed the changes of seasons in Minnesota.

She closed her eyes.

She didn't know what to do with herself. She had no direction, and a part of her had no desire to live anymore. She had joined her life with Paul's and now that part of it was gone. What was left, she didn't like. None of it had meaning. She realized that what she had done with Paul was the only worthwhile thing she had ever done. Now in her late twenties, she wanted to continue doing meaningful things but wondered what to do now that the book was finished. She was out of work and, with Paul gone, out of true friendship.

Exhausted, she drifted to sleep. She didn't even hear Brian's loud SUV pull up.

"Christy?" he said, touching her shoulder.

She jumped. "What? Oh, Brian." She sat up and took a drink of her cold coffee. "I guess I dozed off."

Brian held a white envelope. He sat next to her, looking down, his elbows resting on his knees.

"Brian, what's wrong?"

"Oh, nothing... it's just hard to be here knowing Paul's gone. He was one of my best friends."

"Mine, too."

"Here... this is for you. Paul wanted me to give it to you when he was gone." He handed her the envelope. "And he wants you to open it alone in a safe place."

Christy's eyes watered and she tried to joke, "He has to get the last word, doesn't he?" She tried to smile.

Brian gave a half smile back. "So what are your plans?"

"Well, thanks to you, I got that apartment. I have all of Paul's equipment, so I guess I'll try to find work. Several people I'd met through Paul were at the funeral and talked to me about some work."

"I'd take it easy for a while, give yourself a break," Brian said. "You did a great job for Paul. He was proud of you."

Christy didn't say anything.

"You know, I got a new boat. She's ready..." he paused and tried to smile. "I mean, he's ready to go if you ever need to get away. Just give me a call. You still have my numbers right?"

"Memorized." Christy knew she probably wouldn't see Brian again. That, too, made her sad. She felt Brian would remind her of Paul and she couldn't take that, not now. "You know, Brian, we became pretty close too, didn't we?"

"Yeah, we did." He sniffed and his eyes began to water. "Christy, I lost Paul and I don't want to lose you, too."

"You won't, Brian, I just need some time. I have to figure things out."

"Can I have your number?"

"When I get a phone, sure."

"OK, well, I'll leave you alone. I hope I hear from you soon," he said and stood up to leave.

"You will. I'll call you." Christy knew she'd never call him and she felt bad for lying. It reminded her of guys she'd been involved with before, how she would promise to call but never did. And if they demanded her phone number, she'd make one up.

She listened as Brian drove away.

Christy looked at the envelope in her hands and decided to open it. Where she was sitting was as close to safe as she could get. And alone. She'd never been so alone.

She pulled out a plain white sheet of paper with his handwriting on it and unfolded it.

My dearest Christy,

I miss you already and I haven't even left yet. I'm not afraid. In fact, I'm up for the adventure. Please don't cry for me, I'm free. I'm going to be checking in on you, from time to time, to make sure you're happy. If you're not doing well, I'm going to let you know I'm there for you, the way you were always there for me. I'm sorry I had to leave you, I wish I could've stayed. But we would never have met without all of this. So I feel lucky that I was given this gift of AIDS, because AIDS brought you to me. My life was not complete until you entered it. You were the missing piece I was

waiting for and without you I would have died empty. Thank you
for everything you did for me, and for AIDS. You are a true hero
and a tough one, too. I know this was very hard on you, especially
since we became so close. You forced the needed photos even though
it was killing you to do it. Don't think I didn't know. Christy, I
couldn't have done it. You're my hero. Go for your dreams. You'll
go to the top, Christy, because you can't be stopped. I thought I was
good until you came along. You're better because you're so full of
feeling but still tough enough to get the job done. You amazed me
many times.

I hope I've touched your life, too. I was so into this project and
wanting to help AIDS victims, people I do not even know, that a
part of me hurts now, thinking how I often didn't think about the
one person I did know. The one person that did so much for me. I
talked about not wanting to be selfish anymore. And I look back
now and think that maybe I still was. You asked me to stay with
you, you begged, and even secretly medicated me to keep me here. I
failed to see that maybe you needed me."

Christy was crying hard. "That's right, you fucker! I did need
you! I still need you!" she yelled out loud as if talking to Paul.
She put her head down and cried.

A cool breeze brushed against her. She lifted her head
expecting someone to be standing there but she was alone. She
continued reading.

"Well, Christy, I want you to know that I'm here for you, I'll
always be here for you. I love you. Remember you've got a friend.

"When you're down and troubled... and you need a helping hand... and nothing is going right... close your eyes and think of me... and soon I will be there... to brighten up even your darkest night... you just call out my name... and you know wherever I am... I'll come running... to see you again..."

That comforted Christy. She started humming the song and remembering that night on the boat and how they danced. Christy remembered the leaf and how she'd put it into her bag. The same bag that was inside Paul's place with the last of her things.

She stood with the letter in one hand and coffee cup in the other and went back inside. She brought her cup into the kitchen and set it in the sink. Her bag was lying on the kitchen table. She opened that side pocket and looked in. The leaf was still there. She took it out and looked at it closely. It was a yellow color with brown and holes covering it. She gently lifted it to her mouth and kissed it. "I love you, Paul. I miss you."

15.

Christy didn't leave her apartment for weeks. She never did get a phone. For furniture, she had several boxes of Paul's books, camera equipment and props. She knew she wouldn't be there long. She wanted to move away, but she wasn't sure where or when.

Christy hardly ever showered. She had no pride in herself or maybe too much. The only time she left her apartment was to pick up something to eat and occasionally go for short walks to the art galleries and pick out her favorite new artists. She could tell what people thought of her, with her dirty hair pulled back and unclean clothes and smell. She didn't care. She didn't want people close to her.

In her apartment, Christy often sat and stared at the large photo of the man and woman that Paul had taken. Sometimes she'd watch life passing her by through her window, but usually she slept. She never knew the time of day or the day of the week. She was even unsure of the month, but because of the temperature at night, it felt like fall was around the corner. She knew the month changed when the landlord knocked on her door for the rent.

One morning Christy woke early from hunger. She threw on her jacket and went down to the corner diner that was open twenty-four hours a day. Christy had been there often, usually during less busy times. It must have been around 5:00 in the morning. She sat at a booth and ordered scrambled eggs and toast, her usual. While she waited, her attention turned to the TV on the wall. The morning show hosts were talking about Paul's book. Christy's heart ached, but she couldn't stop watching. They called Paul a hero. They interviewed some of the people that were changed by the book, talking about their sex lives before and after seeing the book.

Paul's attorney and publisher were handling the sales and distribution of the books. They said they needed help to get more people to know that the book was available and free, with donations accepted going strictly for AIDS research.

The woman reporter asked about the photographer and where she was now and what she was working on. Paul's attorney answered, "I don't know, nobody knows. Maybe she died when Paul died."

It was true and she hated it. She finished her breakfast and jumped on the first available bus. She asked the driver what day it was and which bus to take to get over to that twenty-four hour Wal-Mart. It was Friday.

She hopped on another bus. It was close to 7:00 by the time she got there. She ran inside and straight to the music. She found a CD player for a hundred bucks on sale, and she grabbed a few CDs, one being James Taylor's Greatest Hits. She then asked to speak to a manager. The store manager walked up to Christy in disgust by her appearance. "Can I help you?"

"Yes, ma'am. I understand you have latex condoms on your shelves, but I need more. Do you have cases of them in back that I could buy?"

"I can do some checking. They are quite expensive, you know?" she said, looking her up and down.

"Yes, that's fine. I'm buying this too." She pointed to her full cart.

"OK... I'll get what I have and meet you up front."

"Thank you." Christy pushed her cart quickly to the bathroom. She went into a stall and pulled her pants down. She had sewn a pocket inside her pants on the right hip where she kept a lot of her money. She was running out but still had quite a stash. She didn't trust her apartment so she kept a lot of her money with her. She pulled out three one hundred-dollar bills and pulled her pants back up.

When she left Wal-Mart she had three fairly large boxes, so she decided to call a cab. When she got home she turned on the music, starting with "You've Got A Friend".

Christy sat still, listened and cried. She started singing the words. Instead of thinking he was singing it to her, she started singing it to him. "Ain't it good to know you've got a friend... people can be so cold... they'll hurt you and desert you... well they'll take your soul, if you let them oh, but don't you let them... You just call out my name... and you know wherever I am... I'll come running... to see you again... winter, spring, summer, or fall, all you've got to do is call... and I'll be there...

yes I will, you've got a friend... you've got a friend, yeah, ain't it good to know, you've got a friend."

She wanted to be there for him. She wanted to finish what they started.

After she'd played the song several times, she put in an Ani DiFranco CD and jumped in the shower.

Christy had a hard time brushing out her hair and even had to cut out some of the knots at her ends. Her hair was curly enough that it wasn't obvious. She had to hunt through boxes to find all her makeup and hair stuff, but she found it. As much as she didn't want to wear makeup, she forced herself to anyway. She also had to find something a little sexy to wear.

She was ready, wearing faded jeans and a little black halter top that showed her belly button and ring. She was acceptable in society's eyes all made up, but she felt like a clown. She threw on her black sandals and grabbed two boxes of Paul's books. They were heavy and she was thankful she only had to walk a block to get to the busy street.

Christy sat on the boxes as if waiting for someone. And she was.

A young man walking by stared at her as he passed.

"Excuse me!" Christy yelled to him.

He turned back around as if hoping she were interested in him, too. "Yeah?"

"Do you think I'm pretty?"

He laughed. "What?"

"Would you be interested in sleeping with me if I wanted?"

"Do you wanna?" he asked and looked around as if looking for a hidden camera or someone watching. He stepped closer. "What, you sell it?"

"No. I just want to know if you think I'm pretty?" Christy asked him.

"Well sure," he answered.

"I have AIDS," she said.

He was shocked. "What!"

"You wouldn't know it, would you?" She hopped off the boxes and opened them. "Will you let me give you a couple things?"

He stood waiting, and she handed him a book and about three condoms.

"What's this for?" he asked.

"This book is about a friend of mine who died of AIDS. Please look at it and pass it on to your friends." She handed him Paul's book. "These are for you. They work. Please make it a habit to use them. And encourage your friends to do the same."

He gently took the condoms and walked away dumbfounded saying, "Thanks."

She watched him flip through the pages of the book until he turned the corner out of sight.

By the time it started to get dark both boxes were empty, so she headed back home. She took the alley so she could get rid of the boxes and check on her car. She hadn't driven for months. She wanted to see if it would start. To her surprise, it did. It was filthy with dirt and pigeon droppings. She left the car running and went into her apartment to get the other boxes. She loaded them into the hatchback, then turned the car off.

Christy added more makeup and replaced her jeans and shirt with a little black mini dress. One of her favorites, long ago. Now she hated it. She felt too thin and out of shape. But that wasn't the problem. She hated the way it hugged her body for all to see, and that's what she used to love. It was so strange to her how she felt so different from then.

She slipped into her black strappy heels a little clumsily and noticed her hairy legs. She didn't want to take the time to look for her razor and couldn't bring herself to shave them anyway. She wondered if men wanted women's legs shaved so they'd look more like children and not like adult women, who have hair just like them.

She grabbed her black, wraparound jacket and keys and went out to her car.

The place wasn't as busy as she had hoped, but the night was still young. Plus, it gave her a chance to get ready. She knew the crowd would pick up.

She parked her car up close to the front door of the club. She pulled the lever to open the hatchback and jumped out of the car. She opened a box of condoms and one of the boxes full of Paul's books. She took her coat off to sit on it on the back bumper.

She wasn't going for the couples, only the groups of men and groups of women. Three women dressed sexily walked toward the front of the club. They were giggling and loud. Christy could tell they had already been drinking.

Christy stood up before they reached the door. "Hi."

They stopped laughing, two of the girls looking her up and down ignoring her greeting. The other said, "Hi." They kept walking to the door.

Before they reached for the door handle Christy quickly asked, "Can I talk to you for a minute?"

The two girls kept walking and went inside the front door and waited. The third stepped over to Christy.

"Hi. I just wanted you to know that I am HIV positive. I got it one night I went out to a club with some friends, had some fun, drank and picked up one of the hottest guys there. We didn't use protection and now my fate is planned out. No marriage, no kids, just death. I have this book to show you what I'll go through and you'll go through if you're not careful. Will you keep it and tell your friends?" Christy handed it to her.

"Sure." She took it. "You really have AIDS?"

"Well, I will eventually. Right now it's HIV."

"I'm sorry."

"It's OK. It's why I'm here." She nodded her head. "Please don't get it." Christy reached over and grabbed a few condoms. "Share this with your friends and these." She handed her the condoms and looked her in the eye. "They work."

She turned around to look for her friends, but they had gone inside the bar already. "Well, thank you. Um... take care," she said nervously and walked in the front door with the book under her arm.

Two older guys came from the side parking lot. They hardly acknowledged her, talking as they passed her.

"Hey, you guys. Can I give you a book?"

"No thanks."

"How about some condoms?"

"Got 'em." They didn't miss a beat and disappeared into the bar.

"Oh, well," Christy thought. A group of five good-looking, young guys were walking her way. "Hey, didn't I sleep with you?" She yelled to the group.

They all started to snicker looking behind their backs to see who she was talking to.

"Who me?" The tall, dark-haired guy asked.

"Yeah."

"I don't think so."

"Are you sure? It was a while ago."

"Well... I don't remember. I don't think so."

Christy couldn't tell if he was just trying to be macho in front of his friends, like maybe he did sleep with this dark-haired, pretty, slightly older woman even though he knew he didn't. Or if he really was uncertain. It didn't matter. The plan was working. "How about you?" She looked at all of them. "Did I sleep with any of you? I kind of got around." Before they could answer, she continued. "I used to hang out at clubs like this with my friends. I'd pick up guys just like you. I'd take one of you home and fuck you all night. Knowing it was a one-night thing, knowing all you wanted was to get laid. Knowing that, I'd try my best to give you my disease, AIDS!"

They all stood with their mouths dropped open and their eyes wide.

"I'm glad none of you were my victims. I don't do that anymore. Here..." She handed out two books and gave each of them two condoms. "Please use them! By the way, the guy in the book... wasn't gay. He was one of my victims. He loved me, go figure!"

Christy knew what she did gave women a bad name, but she cared a lot more about saving lives right now.

Two of the five guys didn't go into the bar. They went back to the parking lot and left.

After giving out several books and many condoms, Christy was asked to leave by the manager. She went on to the next bar.

Sunday morning when Christy woke, the books were gone and so were the condoms. It only took two days and two nights to hand out all the books and condoms.

After buying the condoms and CD player at Wal-Mart, she realized she was lower on money than she thought. She went down to the corner pay phone and called Paul's attorney, hoping he could, would help her find work. He told her she already had work waiting. They made plans to meet for dinner so he could give her all of the contacts who wanted her.

Christy walked away from the payphone and let the sunlight shine on her face. She felt she was coming out of the darkness. She looked up and thanked Paul for being in that diner on Friday morning.

16.

Christy kept busy with her photography, doing the same thing she had done with Paul only with different types of diseases and problems. She turned more toward women, wanting to learn more about women. She wanted to learn more about herself.

She worked on a book on cystic fibrosis. It was a three-part book on an eight-year old girl, a teenager and a twenty-eight-year-old woman who didn't have long to live. It was hard on her, but she kept working, trying to make a difference.

Another book Christy enjoyed doing was about a woman who had fought obesity her whole life and was going to have her stomach stapled. Christy followed her story for close to a year.

She'd done a book very similar to Paul's, but this book was about a woman with AIDS who wrote poetry and short stories about her experiences, pain and feelings along with the photos. The woman had contracted AIDS from her husband.

But not wanting to go through the loss she experienced with Paul, Christy kept everyone at a distance.

One of her toughest was "Dead Whore" when she worked with a prostitute who was trying to get out of prostitution. She was killed before she was able to escape. Christy had many photos of her and was able to acquire the crime scene photos. Christy put the book out as if she were the woman who was killed and wrote this to go with it:

I died at 3:33 this morning. It's kind of strange because while I was still alive, I loved those numbers on the digital clocks. Three threes, maybe because I wanted three babies. I always paid attention to numbers. My favorite was 12:34, one-two-three-four. It didn't matter if it was afternoon or night; I saw it almost every time. I saw it tonight on his dash clock, too. I guess for the last time. I liked 11:11, eleven-eleven, too. But it was 3:33 that was the last time I saw.

I'm not in pain. In fact, I feel pretty good, better than I have for a long time. Kinda light and floaty. Maybe some kind of drug I've taken might be as close to explaining how I feel. I can't believe it's over. I'm not sure yet if I'm happy or sad. If I had some family close, maybe I'd be more upset, or if I had my own family, three kids and a wonderful husband.

I do miss my mom, though. I remember how she used to rock me when I was just a little girl. She used to brush my hair back off my face with her fingertips, sometimes tucking it behind my ear. Her hands always smelled of flowery scented lotion. She was so warm and I guess you could say tender. She was soft. She loved me. Sometimes she read to me, sometimes she just watched TV or listened to music with me. I remember the way the chair creaked when she rocked, putting me to sleep every time. They say if you count things that keep you up at night like the drips of a dripping faucet or loud chirping of the crickets, it will put you in a deeper sleep than ever. Maybe that's how I feel, like I'm in a deep, deep sleep. The rocking chair was one of the greatest gifts my mom ever gave me, besides the times she rocked me in it. Even now, well, I mean before… whenever I needed comforting and peace I went straight to my rocking chair. I wish I was there now.

They covered my body with a sheet. Oh, God, this body. Look what I've done to it. Scars, physical and emotional. I wish only physical. But I guess that wouldn't make sense. How can you have physical scars without having the emotional ones that go along with them? The physical scars never let you forget. And the man and woman who covered me will never let me forget. Laughing while saying, "Another one bites the dust" in the tune of the Queen song. Like they're glad I'm gone. They didn't even know me. But then again who did? Did I even know myself?

Maybe it is for the best. I never mattered to anybody. I was a brush in the dark, like the trains that used to pass behind the house every night when I was little. I wonder what time it was, if it was 12:34 or 3:33. Those nights were hot and we were poor, but I did have my own fan. I used to set it at the foot of my bed on a small stool. When the train would come, I would turn it off so I could hear the clanging of the metal on metal. I liked the sounds. I always wondered if my mom and dad heard it, too. Sometimes, I wanted to go in and wake them up so they could listen to it with me. Or maybe it was so I could crawl into bed with them. I think I woke up every night because of the train. But only in the summer when it was hot and we had the windows open. Many nights I couldn't fall back to sleep, so I'd flip around with my head at the foot of the bed, turn the fan on high, and sing or talk into it. I liked to hear and feel the vibration. Once in a while, my dad came in to tell me to go to sleep. It was hard to sleep in that heat. It must have been for him, too. Some nights he'd sing into the fan with me. Only once I remember mom ending up in my room, too, all of us lying at the foot of my bed singing into the fan.

Even with only a sheet for a cover it was too hot. But I had to have that cover. Sometimes I'd take my pajamas off instead of the sheet. I had this strange feeling that if I wasn't covered with the sheet something would get me. I could have my head, arms and shoulders out but nothing else. That fear stayed with me throughout my life.

But in death, I want the sheet off. I want to scream! I want to kick it off! But I can't...

I hope my dad is waiting for me just inside the gates. I know he's there. He was the greatest man I ever knew. I guess he was an alcoholic, bad one, too. But he found that group of people and his higher power the day I was born. He was drunk the first time he saw me, and cried for the first time in his life. I loved to listen to him tell the story, even the gross part how chunks came out of his tear ducts, snot out of his nose and mouth. What hadn't been used had been blocked, until that day in the hospital. He sat on the floor beneath the viewing window crying, until someone made a phone call and the room filled with men who really cared, men who had been there. Mom and I were lucky. Mom knew the difference, but I never did. She always told me I was her gift from God, and Dad's, too. Many lives changed on that day. He was the greatest man on earth. I only wish he could have stayed longer. I was twelve when he passed away. Many lives changed on that day, too.

Mom was never the same; neither was I. I guess we both felt abandoned by his death, and maybe at the same time we felt abandoned by God. We needed him. He was everything to us. We lived our lives for him and he did for us. When he died, Mom started drinking. A lot of dad's friends tried to help but less and less as time went on. Mom just wanted to kill the pain, maybe kill herself. I came home from school to find her passed out in some strange position in a different location in the house every day. I got strong carrying her to bed. I was scared on every walk home. What would I find? Is my mom going to leave me, too?

She didn't; I left her.

I couldn't take it anymore. At fifteen, I left. There was a party house across town. Anybody was welcome, anytime they wanted to be there. I wouldn't have to take care of anybody but myself. I tried to go to school, but it was hard to get a ride and the walk was long. Even when I did make it, I hadn't done my homework so I was failing my classes. Then, I didn't go back. I shot pool, did a little drinking, tried some drugs. I just hung out with everybody who hung out there, and I did what they did. An older man kept a close eye on me for a long time. He protected me from others who might have wanted to hurt me. I used to pretend that he was my dad and that everything would be all right, until he raped me. That was my first experience with sex and I guess you could say my only experience with sex. At sixteen, I was walking at night from a bar owned by one of the guys who hung out at the house. I was high on drugs. I dropped my purse and all my stuff spilled out onto the sidewalk. I bent over to pick it up when a man pulled over and asked how much. "Fifty bucks," I said trying to be cocky and joking, fumbling with my things. "OK," he said and opened his car door. At this time, I still didn't know what I was doing or what I was getting myself into. I staggered my way into his car, closed the door and off we went to a parking lot. All I really wanted was a ride to the house. When he finished, he opened the back seat door and literally kicked me out. I sat on the cold pavement and cried.

The pavement felt the same as it does now. Or maybe I felt the same as I do now — dead.

I didn't understand what was happening. But that's how it began. It wasn't always that cold-hearted. Sometimes guys really tried to make me feel good like I mattered, like I meant something to them. That was the worst. They would hand me the wad of cash sometimes giving more than I asked for. Sometimes guys gave me nothing at all or maybe a fat lip or black eye. Some took me to nice hotels, others to the back seat of their cars. Of course I became a pro. I knew how to act and what to say. I always acted like I was having a great time and like it was the best sex ever. A nice smile on my face, "I love being a prostitute, greatest job ever. I get to meet such wonderful people such as yourself." Or, "I'm just putting myself through school," would come out, depending on the customer. "I'm lucky; all women should do it." I was numb and screaming on the inside, crying for my mom and dad to save me. Screaming for God to save me. Please! Somebody save me!

Drinking and drugs numbed the pain. And helped kill me at the same time by keeping me from saving myself. What else could I do? The pain was too great. How else could I survive? This is the way it was. This is what my life had become.

The only comfort I had was the rocking chair and whatever substance I could find to ease the pain. And trains, I still had trains. And that's why I was trying to save some money. I wanted to ride on a train. I believed I would one day. I used to come home, sit in my rocking chair and imagine jumping on a train and going wherever it would take me. There, I would meet my future husband who would be a lot like my father. And my mother would be my maid of honor, and my father would walk me down the aisle at our wedding. My husband would love me so much, and I would love him. Maybe we'd open a little shop together for tourists who step off the train. Soon, I'd be pregnant with our first child. Maybe we'd name him Train because if it wasn't for the train we would have never met.

I stood outside. It was kind of chilly, so I just stood back against the wall of the building, hoping a regular would hunt me down. I wasn't enthusiastic about being out, but I wasn't any other night either. Earlier in the day, I actually had the courage to call about the cost of a train ride and I felt strong for doing it. The woman was so nice to me on the phone; she didn't know who she was talking to. And for a minute, I forgot, too. I was more excited than ever. I was so close to taking this trip that I didn't really fit in this life anymore.

But still, I had some money to make in order to take the trip. The trip would be to go see my mom. I had moved away a few years ago to a bigger city. I called once in a while. Sometimes she sounded good; sometimes she didn't. It was the same for me:

sometimes I sounded good; sometimes I didn't. Sometimes I only called because I needed money. Sometimes, because I really cared how she was doing. I told her I was a struggling actress, which was the truth. I acted my way through life, and I believe she knew it was worse than I let on. Sometimes I wished she would have sobered up and rescued me from this hell.

I should have saved myself.

There were people out there who could have helped me. Maybe at certain times in my life they tried. But I wouldn't let them. I guess I was just too stubborn and proud to let them in. How could I? I had become trash. That's how I had been treated and that's how I treated myself.

Why would anyone want to help? And really the only people who would want to help would be other women. How in the hell could they help? The men who should have helped me would rather hurt me. So they always know they are superior to us. What help could I get from a woman when some think I'm the enemy? I don't like being here... I'm the enemy. I wish they would realize that I'm not the enemy. The men who kept me here are, the men who used me and treated me as less than a human. The men who had their power to help me but would rather hurt me.

He lived in a huge house in a valley. When I arrived at the house the thought of stealing crossed my mind, but I knew I was so close to getting out that I didn't want to ruin my karma. The man seemed too young to have so much but I didn't ask questions. Later I realized that it was his parents' home and they were out of town and he still lived at home. He made me lead the way as he directed me down the curvy stairway next to a waterfall and indoor pool.

The waterfall landed in different pools where Koi fish swam and plants surrounded the ponds. I tried not to look impressed, but I felt like I was in the Garden of Eden, it was so beautiful. Why would somebody like him come looking for somebody like me. He was not a bad looking guy, a little strange maybe, but not bad looking. He must have had great parents, successful. Oh, well, let's get it over with. He paid for two hours and the clock was ticking. As we approached the bedroom I started to remove my top. I turned to him to let him watch and I felt the back of his hand like a brick against my face. I fell back against the bed. Oh, God, not one of these. He came after me and hit me again. He had a hold of my hair and pulled at my shirt ripping it to one side. He punched my bare breast again and again. Oh, God! He flung me over to my stomach, pulled my shorts down and climbed on me penetrating my anus, tearing me, ripping me. It felt like a knife going in and out. Oh, God, make it stop! Make it stop! I cried silently hoping he would finish soon. He did. He told me to stay put, so I did. I didn't know if he had left the room or if he was just standing there silent, looking at me. Too much time had passed so I turned and sat up. When I did, I realized that I was bleeding, but I couldn't tell where it was coming from. Blood was everywhere, and he was gone. I stood and tried to find my way out of the bedroom and out of the house. I knew the trail of blood I was leaving behind, but I couldn't help it. I was weak and blacking out. I had to lean on the wall for support. It was suddenly clear to me that he had been stabbing me in my breast not punching me. I made my way to the stairway and I could hear him talking. Please don't let him see me. I took one step at a time. I was almost to the top when a telephone

*crashed into my face and sent me falling back down the stairs. I
lay there bleeding. He stepped over and picked up the phone. He
told whoever he had been talking to that he dropped the phone and
that he'd call them back later. He started raping me again. Before
he finished he pulled me up and threw me over to a white couch in
a sitting area by the pool. He kept punching my face while inside
me. I could see a digital clock on the stereo; it was 3:33. I blacked
out. That is the last part of my life. It happened so fast. I'm not
sure how I ended up here on the pavement. It's probably where he
dumped me. I'm not in pain anymore, but I hurt because I didn't
get a chance to live my dream... a dream that could have come
true.*

Christy, also wrote a different scenario that didn't happen but
she wondered what would happen if it did. She didn't include
this part in the book.

*I got into his car. Already, adrenaline was pumping through my
body, cold and hot tingling, racing heart, mouth watering. I could
tell the moment the car pulled over that he was a married business
man with kids. It excites me to think of the legacy he will leave
behind: the embarrassment, the hurt it will cause his family. Not
because he left them but the way he died, the secret shameful life he*

led. I know they are better off without him because, after all, he was an awful husband and father, just a plain old awful man.

Why else would he be out here looking for me?

Not much talk. We've already established that it will be a blow job for twenty bucks. He drove to a warehouse district not far from where he picked me up. He will be my seventh victim or is it trophy? The dirtiness of this already has him erect. If he knew this was his last moment on earth, would he do anything differently? Would he be with his family begging for their forgiveness because of the fool he's been? Or would he pray to God for more time to make things right? Anyway, it doesn't matter now... "BANG!"

17.

After writing *Dead Whore*, Christy discovered that not only did she enjoy writing but that the story was really her story and maybe other women's as well — just trying to survive, trying to find her way, get her life back.

After each of her books was released, she would go to the beach at dusk to watch for the moon. She wanted to be close to Mother Earth, to other women and to herself. She often felt that she had given birth to her books and though they were about other people, they had everything to do with her. All her life she wanted to continue in some way but never felt capable enough to have children. She felt she would do more damage to her kids than good. Christy was beginning to feel a shift.

Christy sat on the sand and thought about Paul and Brian and AIDS. She thought about her past, she thought about her future though trying to stay focused on the present.

The ocean was calm with a slight breeze stirring its surface.

She was proud of what she had accomplished in her career. She was proud she'd had such a great friend in Paul. She felt good about where she was in her life, but she couldn't stop thinking about Brian. She tried to remove him from her mind by thinking about all that Paul taught her, all the doors that opened for her because of him and how he always seemed to be right, which used to get under her skin. He was right; she would be a working photographer until she didn't want to do it anymore. She couldn't see that ever happening.

Christy wondered if he had been right about Brian.

She lay back onto the sand and whispered, "Paul, what are you doing right now?" She folded her arms under her head and focused on the moon and the sky and listened to the ocean.

Christy wondered if Paul and her mother had met, if they were together watching over her. She also discovered after writing *Dead Whore* that she was angry at her mom. If it had been her mother's time to go, Christy wished she had been killed by a drunk driver or by the paparazzi chasing her or by a strange disease. She was angry that her mother made the choice to leave her. The suicide left Christy so empty and confused.

She thought about how people just check out of their lives, physically or emotionally, they just check out. Become numb. Can't go on. So maybe they drink or take drugs or eat too much or commit suicide. Or for her, she knew she was numb and figured that was why she drank and had so much sex; she wanted to feel something.

Parts of her life started to make sense. She began to understand why she made some of the choices she had made. She felt hungry to learn more.

It would be getting dark soon and she didn't like to be at the beach after dark. So Christy stood, stretched and brushed herself off before heading home.

18.

Christy looked around her apartment. After everything, her personal life was still a mess and she was lonely. Christy knew she had spent her whole life building walls, collecting fears and abusing herself in every way imaginable. But she wanted a chance. She wanted to make things right for herself.

She could not stop thinking about Brian, and she wanted to do something about it. She wanted to see him again, but she was afraid it would bring up too much pain and memories of Paul.

Before Christy had a chance to cry, she stepped into her bathroom to splash water on her face. The second she saw herself in the mirror she burst into tears. "The mirror." She placed her hands on each side of the mirror and dropped her head. She wanted to be close to herself so that when people had to leave her, she wouldn't leave herself. She wanted to pay attention to herself, really take care of herself not like the stubborn independent girl who used to say, "I can take care of myself! I don't need anyone!" She wanted to take *good* care of herself, love herself, and wrap herself around herself and heal herself. She looked back to the mirror and tried to smile.

She missed Paul and she missed Brian. The memory of the last time she saw Brian made her heart ache.

Christy had wanted to call Brian for months but kept putting it off. Today was Brian's birthday so she nervously dialed his phone number, trembling and scared.

"Hello."

"Hi, Brian. It's Christy."

"Yes, I know. You finally got a phone."

"Yeah." She could hear the sarcasm in his voice. "How have you been… Happy Birthday!"

"Thanks. I'm doing OK. I see you are doing pretty good yourself. I have your books."

"Yeah, I'm hanging in. Do you have plans for your birthday?"

"Yes, I do."

"Oh…well I just called to wish you a Happy Birthday…"

"…But I'd change them if I could spend time with you."

Christy's heart leapt with excitement.

"I've really missed you, Christy. What do you say? Would you be up for dinner with me… tonight?" His voice cracked.

Christy could tell he was nervous too. "I've missed you too, Brian. I'd love to see you."

"Great. Can I pick you up around 6:30?"

"That sounds great. And Brian, I'm sorry I didn't call sooner. I've been…"

He interrupted, "Christy, you called today."

"I can't wait to see you."

"Oh, hey. Do you still live in the same place?"

"Yes, I do."

"OK. I'll see you in a few hours. Christy." He paused, "Thanks for calling."

"I'll see you soon. Bye." She hung up the phone and smiled on her way to the shower.

Christy's joy began to shift back to fear. She didn't expect Brian to be so willing to see her, especially on his birthday. She was afraid of leading him on. She wasn't sure why she wanted to see him. All she knew is that she missed Paul, and she had to figure out if she missed Brian.

19.

Christy waited out front because she didn't want Brian to see the way she was living with no furniture and in a dirty apartment. He pulled up and got out of the car. He walked up to Christy and gave her a hug. She hugged him back. He smelled good and looked even better. "You got a new car."

"Yep. I was tired of the loud green beast. This smaller car feels like a go-kart." He turned and opened the car door for Christy.

"You don't have to open the door for me, Brian."

"I know, Christy." He smiled at her and walked around to get in the driver's side.

"I didn't get you anything for your birthday."

"Yes, you did."

"Brian, we are just having dinner. We are catching up."

"Christy, I've been waiting a long time for this. I wasn't even sure it would ever happen. I'm not going to let you get away from me until I tell you everything I need to tell you."

Christy wanted to tell him not to. She didn't want to hear it. She felt a lump in her throat and said nothing.

Brian kept driving.

"Brian, you don't even know me. You think you do, but you don't."

"Christy, I know everything about you! Everything! You think you're the only one who had nice little talks with Paul. I had talks with Paul, too."

"What do you mean? You're just saying that to get me to talk, and it's not going to work. Paul wouldn't…"

"Paul told me the day he met you, he knew you were perfect for me and that I was perfect for you. So we talked about you a lot." Brian looked over at Christy. "A lot." He smiled.

"So?"

"So, I'm sure you know stuff about me, too."

"Yes, I do. I know you've had eleven lovers… maybe more now."

"Yeah, and I know you don't know how many lovers you've had and that you haven't been with anyone for over maybe three years now… but maybe you have lately."

Christy said nothing.

"I know about your married guy and your service guy. I know about your bulimia and breast reduction."

"Yeah, well I know about your last girlfriend who cheated on you and gave you chlamydia and about your car accident when you were nineteen and that your best friend died in the passenger seat."

"OK, Christy." He shook his head in what seemed disbelief that she knew. He pulled the car over. "I'm sure you know everything about me, all my dirty little secrets." He turned to her and took her hand. "But I need to know if you could love me… could you love me?"

Christy looked into his eyes. She opened her mouth to say yes but nothing happened, no sound. She so badly wanted to experience love.

"Christy, I love you and I think we could have a really good life together. Please let me love you."

"Brian, we haven't seen each other for months!"

"I don't care. My feelings for you haven't changed."

"Why are you doing this? Why right now, so fast?"

"Christy, I've missed you. I've really missed you."

Christy reached over to hug him, still fearful that he didn't know the extent of her past. She wanted him at that moment more than she had ever wanted anybody in her life. She wanted to feel his body on top of hers. She wanted to stay close to him. She wanted to be with him forever.

When they broke apart, Brian had tears in his eyes. "Can we do this? I'm not asking for us to try. I'm asking if we can really do this."

Christy nodded her head. The moment took her by surprise. She knew she would back out later when she wasn't sitting right next to him, smelling him, listening to him, feeling him.

Brian wiped his eyes. "OK, then, that means you're my girlfriend." He gently nudged her and smiled.

Christy giggled and said, "Then I guess you're my boyfriend." She reached for the visor mirror to check her mascara. "I've never had a boyfriend before."

Holding her hand, Brian drove to the restaurant.

After dinner they went back to Brian's house and lay on the bed making plans for the weekend. Christy could see his hard penis through his pants. It made her very uncomfortable, but she couldn't stop looking at it. Her mind was racing trying to figure out how to tell him that she has never been tested.

"Christy, do you want to make love?"

"I have to go." She sat up and looked for her shoes. "Don't get up, I'll call a cab."

Brian put his hand on her back. "Christy, slow down. You can say no."

"Brian, I'm just not ready."

"OK. That's fine. I wasn't sure so I thought I'd ask… I saw you looking at… well you know," Brian gave her a reassuring smile.

Christy relaxed and smiled back, embarrassed. She grabbed a pillow and gently hit him with it. "I'm sorry, I couldn't help it." She paused. "Brian," She took a deep breath and closed her eyes. "I've never been tested."

"I know that, Christy. But it doesn't change anything. It would only change the way we make love. We'd have to be careful."

"You would still want to be with me?"

"Christy, I am with you. Remember what I said. We're doing this, we're not trying to do this, we are doing this."

Christy didn't know if she believed it or not, but she knew she wasn't ready either way. "I'm just not sure. I'm not ready."

"It's OK, Christy. Will you spend the night with me anyway?"

"Can I control the remote?"

"Yes."

"OK, I'll stay."

Brian grabbed her and gently pushed her on the bed. He leaned on top of her and kissed her. "I love you, Christy. Thank you for calling me. Thank you for the best birthday of my life."

20.

The next morning Christy woke early. Brian was asleep next to her. She turned and watched him sleep. She really loved him. She really did. But she was so afraid to be with someone. She didn't know how. What if she felt trapped? She didn't want to feel trapped. She already said she would do this with him, that they would be together. Was it in the heat of the moment? Did she really want to be with him? And what is wrong with him? Why would he want to be with her even if she had AIDS? Who would do that? She became suspicious.

His mouth was slightly open and she wondered if he had bad breath. She leaned forward to take a whiff. "Hum," his breath smelled like corn, like creamed corn. "Corn's good," she whispered to herself. "I like corn."

"You want some corn?" Brian said without opening his eyes. Then he smiled and opened one eye, then the other.

Christy started laughing because she felt like such a dork. "No," she giggled. "I don't want corn right now." She sat up and leaned against the headboard grabbing a pillow to hug in front of her. All her doubts about him drifted away. "You're funny, Brian. I didn't know you were so funny."

"I'm happy, Christy. I didn't know I could be so happy."

"I am not responsible for your happiness, Brian."

"OK, here we go…"

"What?" •

"Christy, are you happy right now?"

She looked up for a second then answered. "Yes… I am."

"Well then, let's be happy together."

"Brian, I just don't want you to get your hopes up, that this will be easy. I don't know how to be in a relationship and… I'm scared. And that scares me to even admit to you that I'm scared. I'm afraid of feeling trapped or becoming somebody else or even being vulnerable around you, yet I feel so vulnerable around you. I don't like it…"

"So don't do it," Brian interrupted. "But don't forget, I've seen you vulnerable. I've seen you strong. You've seen me vulnerable, and I hope you've seen me strong. Christy, we are human. I love you strong. I love you vulnerable. But you need to be who you are. I'm not responsible for changing that in you."

Christy got a little cocky and said, "You can't change that in me!"

"…and you can't make me happy." He reached his hand out to shake hers. "Truce?"

"Truce." She shook his hand.

He gently pulled at her hand guiding her to come closer. She did and snuggled in letting him spoon her. He was warm. He felt safe. His arms were large around her. In her mind she prayed, "God, please don't let me have AIDS."

Christy showered in Brian's master bathroom after him. She reached for the bar of soap. There was a dark brown chest hair stuck to it. It bugged her at first, but then she started thinking about how that same bar of soap had just rubbed all over Brian's body, and now she would rub it all across hers. She was glad they didn't shower together. She was glad he didn't ask. Deep in her heart, she wanted to take things slowly, but her heart was racing.

21.

Christy had been away from Brian all week because she had to go out of town for a shoot. She was glad to be separated for a while to find out how she felt about him, and especially how she was feeling about herself. To her surprise, she missed him and she functioned just fine without him. She felt healthy about this relationship thing. Christy had seen too many people she worked with fall apart, become strange, needy while dating somebody. She wouldn't be one of those.

Christy focused on her assignment. She was working with a pregnant celebrity who wanted tasteful nudes of her and her husband. She wondered if she would ever be able to have a baby. She knew she would never try if she were HIV positive. Then she wondered if she wanted children at all. It was something that she and Brian hadn't talked about.

The new family Christy was shooting gave her butterflies because they seemed so happy and in love. Christy knew she had to be tested because her life was on hold and would be until she did it. How would she do it? Should she go with Brian, or should she go alone? Christy knew that it didn't matter what Brian said, she would not be with him if she had it. She would stay alone and keep working. Unlike Paul, she would take the medication and try to prolong her life but, like Paul, she would try to reach out and help others, maybe by speaking at high schools and colleges about HIV and AIDS.

Her heart sank thinking that she might not have Brian in her life. She thought about the last two weeks with Brian; everything he said to her, the times he made her laugh and the way it felt to be held by him. She didn't want to lose him.

After her photo shoot was over, Brian picked her up at the airport and they headed to her place. She was very nervous for him to see her apartment. They would only be there long enough for her to unpack and pack an overnight bag because they were going to spend the night on Brian's boat.

Christy tried to convince him to stay in the car. "It will just take me a second."

"I'd like to help you with your suitcase and equipment."

"OK."

They walked in the front door and she turned to him. "This is it. This is where I live." She shrugged her shoulders in embarrassment.

"Yes, I know. I helped you find it, remember?"

"Yes, I remember, but I…"

"You have no furniture."

"I know." Christy started to cry. "I miss Paul. When I'm here, I can't stop thinking about him. I can't function right." Her jaw ached from clenching her teeth trying not to cry. "I want him back with me!" She raised her hands to cover her face.

Brian held her in his arms. "Shh, it's OK," he crooned stroking her hair and letting tears run down his face. "I miss him, too."

Christy held onto him.

"Christy, maybe you should move in with me. There's plenty of room for both of us. I don't want to see you living like this, and we could finish the guesthouse for you to set up your studio there."

Christy wiped her eyes. "Brian, I think I have some unresolved issues I need to take care of before we keep moving forward."

"OK, so take care of them. Waiting and worrying will not change the outcome. Wouldn't you like to get on with your life, Christy?"

"I will, Brian. I will. I promise."

"Christy, we could go to the lab right now and I could draw the blood. Then we could head out on the boat overnight. One more night of waiting and we'd have all the answers."

"I need more time. I need to prepare."

"Christy, you're killing yourself worrying about it! I can see what it's doing to you. This is not for me, Christy! Because it doesn't change how I feel... I don't think you have it anyway."

"Yeah, well I do. And it's not you going through it, it's me! I'm the one who has to deal with the possibility of not having a normal healthy life. Not you! Me! And I'd like to know why you would want to be with me if I do have it. I can't understand that."

"Christy, I fell in love with you a long time ago." He paused. "Let me put it to you like this. Imagine we are married and happy. You don't have HIV and I don't have HIV. We are healthy. Then one day, I am working on a patient with AIDS. I draw blood on him, he jerks and the needle goes into my hand. Three months later I'm HIV positive. Would you leave me?"

"No." Christy's eyes watered. She looked down. "I understand."

"Can we go on the boat now?" He looked around the room. "And will you move in with me?"

"The boat, yes. Moving in with you, no."

"Fair enough, let's go."

Christy went into the bathroom where her clothes were in boxes and all over the floor. She grabbed a few things, stuck them in an overnight bag and headed back to the living room. She opened her suitcase from her trip and grabbed her bathroom bag. "I'm ready."

Brian was looking at the photo of Paul's, and he turned to look at her. "I'm sorry if I'm rushing you. I don't mean to."

Christy dropped her bag and gave him a big hug. He lifted her up and she wrapped her legs around his body.

22.

Once they anchored the boat where they would spend the night, Brian and Christy went down below to the bed. They both knew there would be more than talking on this night. There was no TV for distraction.

They lay down facing each other, holding hands between them looking at one another in the dim light. Neither said a word.

He moved a little closer to her. "I want to make love with you, Christy."

Christy's heart started to race. "I want you, too. But Brian, I'm not ready."

Brian inched closer. "We won't then." He rested his hand just below her breasts. "Can I kiss you?"

"Yes." Her breasts were aching to be touched.

He leaned in and gave her a warm gentle kiss on the mouth. When he pulled away, he was smiling. Christy smiled too.

"Do you want children?" Christy asked.

"You want to talk about this right now?"

"No."

"Me neither." He kissed her again.

Brian moved on top of her. She loved to feel the weight of him. His penis was hard and she couldn't control herself. She was dying to be touched and she was dying to touch him. Lightheaded and out of breath, she forgot about everything. She felt healthy, beautiful, desired and worthy of love.

Brian's mouth moved down to her neck. He was gentle and strong, moving slowly.

Christy grabbed his hair in both hands and gently pulled as she moaned. Her hands moved down his back and tried to reach for his ass. She pulled the bottom of his shirt up to get it off of him. He raised his arms to help.

He came back on top of her but with one hand between them. He was holding her breast and teasing her nipple through her shirt.

Christy could feel the hot flood between her legs. She couldn't take it anymore. "This isn't fair," she moaned.

He released her breast and kissed her mouth again. "Are you OK?"

"No, I'm not. I want you so bad. Oh my God, Brian. We have to stop!"

Brian rolled off of Christy and took a deep breath.

She turned to face him, expecting to see anger. She was prepared to apologize, but he was smiling.

"It's going to be amazing," Brian said and turned his head to face her, "when it happens."

Christy giggled with relief that he wasn't pressuring her. "Yes, it will be." She glanced down to see if he was still hard. "Are you OK? Do you need to go use the bathroom or anything?"

He started laughing. "What are you trying to say, Christy? You think I should go use the bathroom?"

"Well, if it would make you feel better."

"I feel just fine." He said and pulled Christy on top of him. "Maybe you need to go use the bathroom?" He laughed.

"I do kind of need to use the bathroom. I should clean up."

"God, I love you Christy. You are amazing."

Still on top of Brian she lay her head on his chest and listened to his heart beat. "Do you want kids, Brian?"

Brian took a deep breath and started playing with Christy's hair. "You know, sometimes I do. But then other times I'm just not sure. Don't get me wrong, I love children. I'm just not sure. My career keeps me busy. I'd want to be a good dad. How about you, do you want to have children?"

"I guess I'm kind of like you. Sometimes I think I would like to have children, but then I think about my mother's life and my life, and I'd be so afraid of doing a bad job as a mother."

"I think you'd be a great mother. Who knows, maybe we will want kids down the road."

Christy kissed his chest.

"If you could go anywhere in the world, for like a honeymoon or something, where would you want to go?" Brian asked.

"I think a cruise would be fun. Or another country would be cool, France, Greece, Ireland. How about you?"

"A cruise would be great. Maybe a European cruise."

"OK. If you had only one month to live, what would you do with the rest of your life?" asked Christy.

"I'd let doctors test every drug possible on me to cure whatever it was I had... I'd spend it making love to you... I'd spend it with you. And you?"

"Well, I'd have to get some crazy photos of the journey. And I'd want to spend it with you."

Brian started laughing. "I have one."

Christy could feel him laughing beneath her. "OK, funny man, what is it?"

"What's up with you and Lucky Charms?"

"Paul told you that?"

"Yeah, he was kind of mad at you. That was his favorite cereal. I can't tell you the number of times he'd ask me to swing by the store to pick up a box."

"Ugh. I don't like the leprechaun."

"Why?"

"Brian, that leprechaun is scary. His eyes freak me out!" Christy sat up to look at him. "They look like devil eyes. That little leprechaun knows something about everyone of us who buys that cereal. It's freaky."

"Christy, it's a cartoon."

"Brian," Christy looked at him in all seriousness, "this is not negotiable."

"I'm not trying to negotiate anything. I heard about it, and I've been dying to ask you about it. And I can see now that Paul wasn't kidding. But boy, did we have some good laughs about it."

"I'm glad you guys had so much fun at my expense."

"You get very upset about the leprechaun. I just think it's kind of funny. I've never seen anything like it…" He burst out laughing again.

"Brian, please. Is that leprechaun on this boat?"

"No, Christy. And it's not in our house either. I don't eat that cereal."

Christy lay her head back down and relaxed. "It's not funny."

"Christy, how long have you had this obsession?"

"I don't know. My mom told me that when I was little she brought home a box of Lucky Charms, I threw a big fit, and the box was never in our house again. She used to take the cereal out and put it in a Tupperware. I like Lucky Charms a lot, but I can't even walk down the cereal aisle."

"Paul told me about your mom. Do you want to talk about it."

"No, there's really nothing to say. What about your parents?"

"They are alive and well and live in Orlando."

"How about your friends? What are your friends like?"

"Well, most of my friends are from work. The majority of my friends are male, but I have a couple of close female friends I work with. Both are married and both were getting very tired of hearing about you. Since you called me for my birthday, they are a little more interested. So thank you for calling me, Christy; I have an interested audience again."

"You're welcome. And the guy friends?"

"They never really were great listeners. They just wanted to take me out and get me laid. Their wives were even in on it trying to set me up with women. They thought they could get me over you."

"I don't understand… I didn't know how you felt. I knew there was an attraction for both of us, but I thought that's all it was."

"Not for me. I thought you were something special the first day I met you, but it wasn't until we took Paul on the boat that I knew I had fallen for you."

Christy shook her head in disbelief. "I really didn't know."

"At what point did you become quote – unquote 'attracted' to me."

"I was…" Christy raised her hands to make the quotes, "'attracted' to you that first day I met you."

Brian chuckled.

"The boat. It was when we danced on the boat I could tell I felt something. But I… just… you know…"

"And here we are on a boat and when we have our honeymoon, we'll take a cruise on a…"

They said "boat" together.

"Maybe boats should be our thing."

Christy stood up and reached out her hand for his. "Maybe dancing on a boat should be our thing."

Brian held her close to him they swayed to no music.

After about five minutes, Brian broke the silence. "You didn't tell me about your friends."

"I don't have any. I never really have."

"How is that possible? No friends?"

"I don't know. Paul was my first friend… and you. I'd like to have some female friends. Can I have yours?"

"No, you can't."

"Well that's not very nice. You have a lot of friends; you could spare a couple friends."

"You can borrow them, but you can't have them."

"Oh, all right."

"I'm sure you've met people through your work, haven't you?"

"Yes, but honestly, Brian, with a guy I don't know if he wants to be friends or if he wants something else, so I just stay away. I keep it professional. I've been invited out with a couple women a few times, but I just don't know what I'd have in common with them. I don't know how to have a female friend. I've heard all the little comments that women are catty and jealous, that women are always in competition with each other. I wouldn't want any of that."

"I've always known women to have much better relationships than men, healthier, more solid than guys. So I don't know where you get that other stuff from."

"I don't know either. The media?"

"That's where I'd put my money. Really, Christy, give those women a chance."

23.

The next weekend Christy went out with a woman she met on a shoot, a make-up artist named Lisa. Lisa brought along a good friend, Angie, who was a writer for a women's newspaper. The three went to a little jazz club and had a drink. Then they walked across the street to a coffee shop where they talked until it closed at midnight.

Angie was in town doing a story on human trafficking. Christy was intrigued. Even though she walked with a limp and her left hand didn't seem to work quite right, Angie was beautiful, with something about her that made Christy want to know her better. She wanted to take photos of her. There was a strength to Angie that she had never seen in a woman before, or a man.

After Lisa left, Angie invited Christy to her hotel room for a cup of tea and to fill her in on some of the work she was doing. Angie told her that she had been shot and she was still in speech and physical therapy. Angie felt she would make close to a full recovery.

"Who shot you?"

"Long story." Angie looked up from her tea at Christy. "You really want to hear this?"

"Yes, I really do."

"OK. I got together with some friends and we took over a strip club. We made all the men get naked and dance for us."

Christy sat with her mouth open, and then she started to laugh.

"It's not that we wanted to see them naked, it's that we wanted them to know what it felt like." Angie started laughing too. "Trust me, a year ago, I would never have thought I'd be laughing about it today."

"Why? I mean how did…? What…?" Christy nervously laughed again.

"OK, I'll start from the beginning. I had a rough life. I got myself together and started working for a women's newspaper; same place I still work. They've been so good to me. I'm actually an owner now." She took another sip of her tea. "Anyway, I wanted to do a story on women who work in a strip club. So I did. I hated how the men treated the women, and I wanted to encourage the women to make changes to improve their lives."

"The owner shot you because you were taking all his women away?" Christy questioned.

Angie laughed. "Sounds like a good story, but nope. My best friend, Julie, is as feisty as they come, and she joined in and a group of us women… Julie kind of ran the show. Anyway, we took over the club and made the men take all their clothes off and dance for us."

"Oh, my God, you are my hero!"

"It sounds good, but it wasn't. It was horribly sad. It doesn't take much to persuade people to treat other people badly."

Angie put her head down then looked at Christy. "Just power. That's it, power."

"That's profound."

"Not really, that's what all sexual abuse is and has always been about — power."

"I guess you're right."

"There was a bad cop there that night and I got shot by him." Angie looked down. "It's been tough. It should have been a perfect ending to an imperfect life... but I lived. I really can't believe I lived."

Christy moved over to Angie and sat next to her placing her hand on her back. "Angie, you don't really feel that way do you?"

"No." She shook her head, then grinned. "It has made me more angry and ready to fight for women and children. Today, I have more power and the written word. And I want to use it in a good way. I want to educate and help others."

"You are incredible. Do you realize that?" Christy asked. "Why didn't I meet you before? I mean, we're both from Minnesota. How could I not know about you..."

"I think the media kept it pretty quiet."

"Maybe the bar owner paid them off," Christy added.

"The thing is, everything just got way out of hand. Everybody was going through the rush of adrenalin, emotions were crazy, the men and the women. We just wanted to change the men's perspectives."

"You're OK, though? Are you OK?"

"Yes, I'm great. Still trying to change perspectives, still fighting for women."

"High five!" Christy raised her hand and Angie returned the high five.

"I can't tell you how inspired I am right now. My photography is moving in that direction, focusing more on women. And I love it." Christy lifted her cup of tea. "I think it's my calling." She took a sip and set her cup down. "It's strange. I've always hung around men, always tried to stay close to men. I cared more about what men thought and wanted than what I thought or wanted or what women thought or wanted. Until now. Now I care. Now I want to know what I want, what you want," She looked at Angie. "What other women want and even what children want. I haven't had girlfriends since high school and even then I was so awkward and insecure I still spent more time with the boys."

"Sounds familiar. We try to convince ourselves that we have nothing in common with the girls and women in our lives and that these guys are our best friends but..."

"I wonder if it has anything to do with how so often in school we only learn about men making history, and if you are an inspired, ambitious, goal-oriented young woman with ambitions..."

"Who can you look up to?"

"Exactly!" Christy drank the last of her tea. "I'm so glad I met you."

"Me too. You have got to meet my best friend Julie. You'll love her."

"I'd love to meet her. I could use all the friends I can get, female friends. I can't get over what I've been missing out on, not having girlfriends."

"I was the same when Julie came along for me, exactly the same. So anyway, what are you working on next, for women?"

"You know, it's strange. My work is going well. It's my personal life that needs help." Christy decided to blurt it out. "The next thing I'm working on is trying to find the courage to get tested for HIV. I've never been tested. And there have been many men, many."

"I understand." Angie sat quietly.

"I haven't been with anyone for about three years, and now I have this great man who wants to be with me either way. But I wouldn't, I couldn't be with him if I have it."

They sat quietly. Angie finished her tea and set the cup back on the table. The silence was appreciated by Christy. She didn't know what Angie was thinking, but it didn't feel judgmental or like pity. It felt like honest concern. Christy felt safe.

"Baby steps, Christy. Let's go tomorrow and get the info on getting tested. I'll go with you."

Christy smiled and shook her head slowly. "I don't know."

"This huge thing is holding you back. Let's break it up into small steps."

Christy sat silently thinking about all the ways it has held her back. Every aspect of her life has been affected by this not so simple test. "OK, let's do it."

"Great!" She leaned over and gave Christy a hug. "What a great night! What a great woman you are!"

"You're awesome, Angie!" They broke their hug. "Well, I have a big day ahead of me I better get home and try to get some sleep."

They stood, stretched and headed to the door to say their goodbyes and schedule a time to meet in the morning.

They agreed that her decision to be tested had absolutely nothing to do with Brian. Angie and Christy would meet at a clinic the following morning to get more information on getting tested — just information, no more. How do they draw the blood? How long does it take to get the results? What should she do while she waits? Are there support groups? What is the next step if Christy is HIV positive? Do they offer counseling?

When Christy got home, she was so excited she called Brian and woke him up.

"Hi, honey, sorry to wake you, but I just wanted you to know that I'm home now and I had a good night. Thank you for encouraging me to find girlfriends."

"That's OK. I'm glad you had a good time."

"OK. Well, goodnight."

"Goodnight, honey. I love you," Brian said before he hung up.

Christy rolled over, set her alarm and snuggled in under the covers for the rest of the night. She wished she had a bed. She wondered if sleeping on the floor was good for her back. She drifted off to sleep.

24.

When Christy woke she was excited about taking this first step. She knew it was the right thing not to include Brian because this was something she needed to do alone. She wanted to surprise Brian and, because her life was so good, it became harder and harder to believe that she could have it.

At the clinic, Christy got all the answers she was looking for and without a second thought said, "Can I get tested right now?"

"Me too?" Angie added.

"I don't see why not." The nurse said and went to get the forms.

Christy and Angie didn't say a word until after the test was completed and they were headed to their cars. "Thanks for joining me, Angie."

"Thanks for joining me, Christy."

They smiled and hugged.

"I hope you don't take this wrong, but I'm going to need this time to be alone. I have two days of waiting..."

"Perfect, because I'm out of the country for four days. I'll call you when I get back."

"OK."

Christy was on an emotional rollercoaster — happy she did it but terrified, thinking that she didn't have it, then knowing that she did. She cried as she drove home.

The next two days she avoided Brian's calls and left messages on his machine when he was at work so she didn't have to talk to him. She stared at Paul's cologne photograph and listened to "You've Got A Friend." She thought about her past. She tried to make a list of all her lovers, but it only depressed her because she couldn't remember names.

Mostly, she slept.

It was time. Christy sat in the office and waited for the nurse to bring the results. She was sweating and shaking and felt like she had to go to the bathroom. She waited.

The nurse walked in and sat down. She opened Christy's chart and took a look. "The test was negative. Do you have any questions?"

"Does that mean I don't have it?"

"Yes, that means that you tested negative for HIV." She closed the chart. "I didn't mean to spring it on you so fast. It's just that I don't like to make patients wait. It's hard enough to wait the two days."

"Yes, I'm a little stunned. I didn't expect the answer so quickly. Are you sure?"

"Yes."

Christy started to cry. "Now what should I do?"

"The test is negative. You don't have HIV," the nurse reassured Christy.

"OK." Christy kept crying as she stood up.

The nurse reached out and gave her a hug. "Are you OK?"

"Yeah, I am."

Christy drove straight home. It became very clear to her that she had plans if she was HIV positive but she didn't have plans if she didn't have it.

She grabbed the Yellow Pages and began searching for a counselor. She called several offices before she found a counselor who actually took her call. Christy liked her immediately. She was firm and to the point, and that was exactly what Christy wanted because she didn't want to waste time. They set up the appointment for later that afternoon.

25.

After signing the confidentiality papers, Mary started off with, "I'm not the typical therapist. I want you in and out. I don't want this relationship to go on longer than it has to. We will talk. I will listen, but if I hear you talk about the same problem more than twice, together we will come up with an action to solve it. I'm all about actions, and I have an action plan I use for everybody. It works. It's the same formula, but it turns out to be different for everybody. Any questions?"

"No."

Mary went on to tell Christy about her education, the books she'd co-authored, places she'd worked and studies she'd been part of.

Christy decided she wanted to know the formula before she confided in her.

"It's simple. Three-four-two are the numbers to remember. Three ways to release unwanted baggage, four keys to happiness and two must-follow rules in finding the love of your life... yourself."

Then it was Christy's turn. "I don't want to waste time. I want to work hard and I think your formula hits on what I'd like to deal with." Christy told her everything from her mother's death to her new relationship with Brian. She talked about her modeling and body image, especially her breasts. Christy talked about her bulimia and cutting, her not having friends and the love she had for Paul. They talked about AIDS and how Christy didn't have it even though she thought she did because of her past carelessness. Christy unloaded everything and it felt great.

When she left Mary's office, she felt so strong and happy that she headed straight over to the hospital to talk to Brian. She walked into the hospital and down the hall to the back office where he often was. He was standing in the hall talking to a doctor. He turned and looked at her. He stopped talking and started walking toward Christy. Sensing something was wrong, he grabbed her hand and led her into the office, closing the door.

"Are you OK? Are you sick?"

"No, Brian. I'm not. I was tested two days ago and I just got my results. It's negative."

He gave her a huge hug. "That's great news!"

"I'm mixed up, and I need a little time. I really thought I had it. I really did."

"OK, take your time, Christy."

"Brian, I need to be clear about something. I want to be with you. I love you. But I need to stay where I am for a while. I need to spend time focusing on me, my career and my future with you in it. I need to get to know you better. I know you are a great man. I know your heart, but I really don't know you very well. I'd like to meet your friends, your family. I want to court."

"You want to court?"

"Yes, I want to court... that's the word, right? I want to date. I want to become best friends. I want a strong foundation."

"I already know you, Christy. I know you are the one for me."

"But Brian, you really don't know me because I don't even know myself."

Brian put his head down. "OK, Christy, if that's what you need. Nothing changes for me, I feel the same."

"So do I. Brian, you're missing the point. Nothing changes for me either. I just need time. I want to date you... I don't want to move in with you."

"Is that what this is about? You don't want to move in with me?"

Before Christy could answer...

"Christy, you don't have to move in with me. God, Christy, come here." He reached for her and gave her a hug. "I didn't mean to pressure you. I just hate seeing you live where you do, in its condition."

"I'm going to clean it up. I'm headed home now to get started."

"Can I help?"

"No thanks, Brian. It's my mess." She meant that for every part of her life. It was her mess, and she was going to clean it up.

26.

Christy sat on the floor in her main room going through boxes. She thought a lot about everything Mary and she had talked about. Mary had asked her if she felt like she had control over her life. That was a hard one for Christy to understand. Who else would be controlling her life? Christy began to understand when she talked about boundaries and being clear about the things she wanted and didn't want. She sent Christy home with a fancy pen and journal to write down any thoughts, questions or things she'd like to talk about at their next session. Her homework was to start cleaning her apartment.

Christy wrote in the journal that she was tired of her breasts feeling strange and she was tired of feeling strange about breasts. And before discussing it with Mary, she took action. She grabbed the Yellow Pages again and found a massage therapist who specialized in lymphedema massage, deep tissue massage and acupuncture. The perfect place to start, she scheduled an appointment for the next day.

Settled back down with her boxes, she felt proud of the steps she was taking. She wanted to move forward with Brian, but she wanted to be not only free from HIV, but emotionally and physically healthy.

The full boxes had no order. Christy felt like it was a waste of time. She was getting nowhere and only finding herself lost in memories, most weren't good memories. She stood up, turned on her stereo and bounced around to the hip-hop music on the radio station. She used her feet to push the junk out of one corner and when she found the bare floor she started throwing all of her clothes there. She went to another corner and cleared it. Anything to do with her photography went there. She started pushing and shoving everything toward the bathroom. She had a pile in the center of the room and went into the bathroom to clear it out. She threw everything from the bathroom into the center of the pile. She grabbed box after box and emptied them on the pile. Then she used the empty boxes for other categories. All of her pictures went into one box. Garbage went into another. Bathroom stuff, she just threw into the bathroom. Things she'd use in the kitchen went into the third box. When she had three boxes of garbage, she went down to the alley to dump them. When she walked back into her apartment she couldn't believe the difference already. She had been sorting without realizing it and the time was flying by.

The phone rang. It was Brian.

"I know this is short notice, but I was wondering if you would be interested in joining me tonight for pizza, beer and football at my place around 8:00?"

"I'd love to." Christy said. "But Brian, you must realize, I really don't like sports."

"But you like me, right? And you like beer and pizza?"

"OK then, just wait till I get my place cleaned up, I'll have you over for sushi and a Lifetime movie."

"You're on!"

When Christy got off the phone, she again was impressed with the dent she had made in her place. She believed the clutter and chaos in her apartment represented the clutter and chaos in her life. The lack of care for her apartment matched the lack of care she had for herself.

Christy sniffed out some clean clothes and jumped in the shower. She was excited to go shopping. She went to the nearby Target to get cleaning supplies and laundry soap. She also picked up a TV, some hangers, a dresser she'd use for clothes and to set the TV on. She found a few other things she wanted but decided to wait until her place was cleaner. Plus, she didn't have room in her car.

Christy showed up at Brian's house carrying a couple of bottles of sparkling water, raspberry flavored she had found at Target. It was the first thing she'd bought for her refrigerator. She explained to Brian that she didn't want to drink tonight. She wouldn't be spending the night because she had an early morning appointment. But the truth was she didn't want to have sex, and her history with drinking and men made her unsure of herself.

Christy found herself inspired by the game, by some of the athletes. She learned how some of the players overcame great odds. She quietly sat eating pizza and watching the players who stood out because of their talent. Christy wanted to be good at something, she wanted to stand out, take chances. Christy wanted to be bolder and braver in her work, in her life.

At half-time, Christy broke her silence. "Brian, I have some thoughts on football."

"OK, Christy." He turned toward her on the couch. "What'cha got for me?"

"I wouldn't mind football once in a while. I hate the commercials, especially the beer ads. They are degrading to women. The other thing I noticed is that in football, men are penalized for holding. I've heard that women like to cuddle and be held by their man. So I'm wondering if some men have become a little mixed up and think that while they are lying on the couch with their wife, they think they are playing football and if they are caught holding their wife, they will be penalized?"

Before Brian could answer she continued, "Brian, you will not be penalized for holding my hand. Just so you know." Christy giggled. "I'm sorry. I just had to take a little jab for the commercials I had to sit through."

"I could take your mind off the commercials," Brian teased.

"Game time! We need two pens and two sheets of paper."

"What for?"

"I want to have a contest."

"OK." He handed her a pen and paper. "What's the contest?"

"Well, while we've been sitting here watching, I've heard many words that could be sexual, so the contest is, whoever writes down the most dirty words heard during one quarter of the game wins."

"Wins what?" Brian had a deviant smile.

"Just wins the contest."

"Well, I'd like to know what I'm going to win."

"You're going to win? I don't think so!"

"If you're not afraid, let's put a wager on it."

"All right, fine. What do you want to bet?"

"Let's see… I'd like a back rub."

"OK, if I win, I'd like you to rub my feet."

They shook hands just before the third quarter began. The game was on. Christy knew she had the advantage, she wouldn't watch the game, she'd only listen for the words. It seemed they were hearing the same words because they kept writing at the same time. But then Brian broke ahead with some Christy wasn't getting. It went back and forth for a while.

Christy didn't want to tease or lead Brian on with this game, but she didn't want to stop having fun either.

"Brian, is this game OK even though we're not having sex tonight?"

"Shhh… Christy, I'm playing a game here."

"Brian."

He leaned over and gave her a kiss. "OK, I'll give you one of mine because it's clear I'm winning… penetration."

"I already have that one."

"Touch."

"Got it."

"Position."

"Got that one too. Should we call it a game and count them up?"

"Sure… I have thirty-nine."

"Thirty-nine?"

"Yeah, how many do you have?"

"Thirty-one."

Brian's shirt came off quick.

Christy started laughing until she was overwhelmed by lust. She didn't even care to recount or debate the words he had. His skin was smooth and tanned. His body was amazing. He would make a great model. Christy had to stop thinking about him like that. She turned it around and started envisioning her own body. She closed her eyes and started at Brian's shoulders.

"How much time do I get?"

"Until the game is over, unless it goes into overtime."

Christy went back to her own body. She rubbed Brian's shoulders the way she would want to be rubbed, deep and relaxing. Charles Cannon would love a model like Brian. She thought about Charles Cannon, the creator of the sculpture of her in Chicago and her favorite modeling job. She loved modeling for him because his wife made these amazing gourmet meals for lunch. Christy always wanted seconds but never took them because she didn't want to appear fat and bloated. It was the best food she'd ever had.

She learned a lot about them as a couple, and she really liked them. They didn't let people in their home with their shoes on. They gave each visitor a pair of slippers to walk around in. Christy always had the pink ones.

Christy remembered in disgust the one day she showed up at their house after a night of drinking and sex. She had slept late and didn't have time to shower. She remembered feeling so humiliated and embarrassed with her tangy smell of sweat and other fluids, and most were not her own. Thinking they could smell it on her, she felt like such a low life compared to this wonderful married couple.

Another modeling job came to her memory, the time she modeled her face. It felt good to know the students were painting her face not her naked body. She felt beautiful, like a real model. Then during one of the sessions the instructor asked her, "How old are you?"

"I'm twenty-seven."

"That's what I thought. OK class, you'll notice how Christy is beginning to show she's aging." She walked over and pointed to Christy's face at the jaw line, almost touching her. "You see here? This is where her skin is beginning to show gravity at work. She still looks good at her age, but it's going to happen just like my face, see how my face appears to have this extra pouch here on both sides of my mouth?" She pointed back to Christy's face. "It's around Christy's age that it starts to happen, people start getting the jowls." Christy didn't even know what jowls were. She had heard it used referring to eighty-year-old men but never a twenty-seven-year-old woman.

Christy was suddenly feeling so ugly that all of her imperfections came flooding to the surface and she wanted to scream out, "Why don't you just talk about all of it! Here, I'll help you! Let's start at the top of my head... I have thirteen gray hairs that I have to pluck out every other week, plus I put highlights in my hair to camouflage any others I might not be aware of. Yes! I'm well aware that I'm aging, damn it! I have wrinkles around my eyes, not to mention my droopy eyelids that almost overlap the outer corners of my eyes which only seem to get worse with age. Oh! And my eyebrows… I don't know what I'm supposed to do with my eyebrows. I have a scar in the middle of my left eyebrow where hair doesn't grow at all… I don't know why you didn't mention my two squinting vertical lines between my eyebrows. And my aging, sagging skin is causing my pores to get bigger and bigger. I have sun damage from not wearing sunscreen, why didn't you mention that? What about that? Oh, and don't forget to point out that I have a mustache, yep, a mustache. Most of it's blond, but on each side the little hairs are brown and noticeable. Wow, maybe you didn't notice that. Well, I guess you don't know everything about my imperfections, do you? I'm not finished. You didn't even mention my big nose and the big pores and blackheads that cover my big nose. You didn't even mention the hair that grows out of it that I have to pluck weekly. Let's work our way down, I have a whisker on my chin that sneaks up on me out of nowhere, that ruins whatever fun I'm having until I can get home and get my hands on tweezers. Below that I have loose skin under my chin maybe you'd like to call it chicken neck. I've heard others call it that, I don't know why exactly. I'm not wearing a turtleneck so unless you're blind you've missed the ring wrinkles around my neck, maybe you thought I was wearing a new style of choker. Moving down, my breasts are beginning to sag along with my butt. I swear to God when I look in the mirror sometimes I think it looks like my butt is sitting behind my knees. Let's see what else I should point out to you since you've overlooked the obvious…Oh, I know. I get acne on my back. Plus, not only is my face sun damaged, but almost every inch of skin is damaged. Oh, except for my butt that rides behind my knees. I've never had kids, yet I have a stomach pouch that just likes to live on this body. Besides all that, you don't know me at all… you students look at my face or look at my body, but do you realize that you're looking at a slut. I'm sure you've heard of sluts, but in case you've never really known one first hand, now you do. I'd like to introduce to you an aging, deformed slut. P.S. I may have slept with one of your husbands! How do you like me now?"

But she didn't. She just thought of all that was wrong with her. Before the class, Christy kind of liked her face. After, she felt like an ugly freak of nature.

Christy tried to pretend that she didn't have a problem with getting older, but she did. She had a problem with the importance of youth in our society. But more importantly, Christy wasn't happy with where she was in her life at her age. She believed she should be further along, successful, settled down, happy.

Christy remembered how she was so self-conscious after that modeling job; she would constantly look in mirrors to check out her jowls and the lines going down between her nose and cheeks. Christy pulled at her face by her ears to see what a facelift might do for her. She could see gravity working on her face.

Before modeling her face, Christy remembered sitting at work looking into a mirror and seeing those lines for the first time. She was thrilled. She was beginning to look like a woman and not so much like a child. She felt like she was finally graduating to being a woman.

Then after some time admiring those lines, she started seeing commercials on TV geared to women. They tell us we have a problem, point it out to us. Then they make us afraid that we are getting old and ugly. But they have good news; they have the product to save us. We no longer have to be afraid. It's crazy making.

Buy our product and erase years from your face. Christy used to have a closet full of those half-used miracle products. If Christy hadn't seen the commercial, Christy wouldn't have been on that thirty-second rollercoaster ride and she wouldn't need to run out and spend money on something because she's so disfigured. It didn't take long before she hated the lines and how her face was starting to look.

She wished she still loved those lines and loved what they stood for, growing up and loving where she was, who she was. Christy knew she wasn't there yet.

She finished rubbing Brian's back and realized how little she thought about her looks these days. Maybe she was getting closer to where she wanted to be.

27.

At Christy's next appointment with Mary, she learned the formula in greater detail. Mary printed off a copy for her. The title at the top of the page read, Mary's Formula.

The first topic was Three Ways to Release Unwanted Baggage. Below it listed: Take full responsibility for your life. Make peace with yourself; forgive yourself. Love your past; turn something hurtful into a gift.

The next topic was Four Keys to Happiness and listed: Give back. Stay true to your values. Balance your time into thirds: one-third self, one-third social, one-third purpose and passion. Demand more from yourself and for yourself.

The last topic was Two Must-Follow Rules in Finding the Love of Your Life…Yourself. Then listed: Be nice to yourself; love yourself. What you need from a partner, you must be willing to give to yourself.

Christy was intrigued by the clear outline and the look of simplicity, but she knew it couldn't be that easy. She compared her life to the formula and couldn't make the connection.

Mary watched Christy as she read through it. "Christy, let me explain how this works. To start with, I can see you are starting to take responsibility for your life. Making the appointment to see the massage therapist, working on your apartment and being clear with Brian that you aren't ready to move in with him are all steps in the right direction.

"You were very clear about what you would have done if you had been HIV positive. That is an example of turning something hurtful into a gift. I can clearly see another, if you don't mind?"

"Sure, go ahead."

"Your mother's suicide turned you into a strong, independent young woman with amazing survival skills. Christy, I believe you could survive anything that comes your way."

Christy started to cry. "Really?"

"Yes, Christy. Really." She handed Christy a box of Kleenex. "I think it's a gift your mother gave you, and I think you should be proud."

Christy wiped her eyes, her heart suddenly felt full. She had never thought about her mother in that way. She had always believed she was abandoned by her mother.

"Now backtracking, making peace with yourself, forgiving yourself can be very personal or you can share it with me. Many clients have done rituals like making a list of all the terrible things they have done, choices they've made and then burning the list to let it go. One man wrote each thing down on the beach and let the waves carry it out to sea."

"Or I could send them away in helium-filled balloons."

"That would work. You can also just list each one and pray on every one of them, pray for forgiveness."

"I understand."

"Now for the giving back, you have got to do something to get out of yourself. You've been self-absorbed at times, haven't you?"

"Yes."

"Though you don't have HIV, why not still do some of what you were going to do if you did? You can speak at colleges. You could go and hold AIDS babies. Just volunteer, get involved in something that will help others. It's a must.

"Now, as far as your values, do you know what they are?"

"Umm, not really."

"Let's quickly give you five right now. I like to keep a top-five list. You can change it as needed, and you can add to it if you want, but always have your top five."

"I value time to myself. I didn't know I did, but I really do. And I value my career."

"That's great, Christy. The next on our list is just about that very thing, balance your time. It's easy when you break it up into thirds: one-third self, one-third social, one-third purpose and passion. So maybe this should be one of your values. You value time with yourself, time for your career and time with Brian and friends."

"I really don't have any friends."

"Don't say that. You have Brian, Angie and Lisa. Believe it or not, you still have Paul. You could go to the cemetery and spend time with him, talk to him."

"You're right."

"What else do you value?"

"I value exercise even though I haven't been taking good care of myself."

"What else?"

"I value art."

"Do you ever go to galleries?"

"No. I haven't for a while." Christy was beginning to see how she wasn't true to her values. She was feeling disappointed in herself.

"What else?"

"I value the time I spend with Brian, but I know that is in with balance."

"You think about this; it will all fit together. You will begin to see what's important to you. Now, the reason we divide our lives into thirds, is so if we have to shift something, or lose something, we haven't lost everything. If your life was only about your work and one day you found yourself out of work, it would devastate you. Same goes for Brian. If your life revolved around a man and one day he decides he doesn't love you anymore, your whole life would fall apart. But if you still have other friends and a wonderful career and enjoy your time alone, you'd be just fine." She leaned in toward Christy. "Do you see what I mean?"

"Yes. It makes perfect sense."

"OK, demand more for yourself, from yourself. I think you are doing well with this one. By giving up on sex and men, you've demanded a good man and he showed up. What do you want from yourself?"

"I'd like the transition into this relationship to go smoothly. I feel like I'm making Brian jump through hoops, and I don't want to do that. I'd like to demand better trust in myself. I'd also like to take more chances with my photography. I'd like to be braver and bolder, tell stories that aren't being told. I know I want to stay in the US to do it. I've seen too many go to other countries when I think we still have work to do here. I don't know if we've become desensitized to our own problems: domestic abuse, child sexual abuse, rape, the homeless, prostitution — there's so much here that maybe I could do something with my work and help at the same time."

"Wonderful, Christy. Wonderful. OK, next is be nice to yourself. I like to add, if you won't, who will? I want you to think about some things you can do for yourself, maybe take a bubble bath tonight. Oh, you are getting your massage today, aren't you? See, you're doing it already.

"The last one is, give to yourself what you need from a partner. This one is important because it keeps us from making too many demands on the people we love. It seems you think you have put many demands on Brian, so now it's your turn to put the same demands on yourself. I think honesty is the place to start. Christy, you can't love somebody else if you can't love yourself. Decide what you want, Christy."

28.

Weeks passed and Christy worked hard. Her place was spotless. She actually discovered that a clean home was one of her values. She bought a bed that also worked as a couch during the day. The massages helped her feel better about her breasts and they even felt healthier to her. It was easier than she thought to make new friends, but Angie was her best friend. They talked on the phone almost every day. She was so inspiring that Christy was starting to take more risks with her photography.

Christy let go of her past in greater detail than the first time. She used the helium balloons, and she released them at the cemetery with Paul. She stopped going to Mary but continued using her formula. She discovered that the balance really covered everything. As long as she kept her balance, she would be OK.

Brian proposed the last time they went to see Paul together and Christy accepted. To Christy, it was the perfect proposal; without Paul, she never would have found Brian. Even though Paul was no longer physically with her, his love was still touchable. She could wrap her arms around herself and still feel his love. And every time Brian hugged her, she felt Paul and Brian loving her.

Brian also got tested for HIV. Though he was a nurse and frequently tested, she felt it best if they were both disease free. And he was. Brian, Christy and all their friends were working on finishing Brian's guesthouse for Christy's new studio. It was looking great, and it was so much fun putting it together with friends.

There was a new exhibition at Christy's favorite gallery, so she headed over to see it. She was so full of anticipation that it was hard to appreciate the work. Tonight was the night that she wanted to make love with Brian. She was ready and couldn't wait. He didn't know. They had plans for dinner then they were going back to her place for a movie. She bought condoms and candles for the occasion.

She thought back over her life. She wondered if her happiness was from God's divine order, or if it really came from her doing the work.

Either way, she was thankful.

If you enjoyed
Touchable Love,
An Untraditional Love Story,
why not try other great titles by
Becky Due?

The Gentlemen's Club, A Story for All Women
Novel $14.95   978-0-9746212-0-3

Touchable Love, An Untraditional Love Story
Novel $12.95   978-0-9746212-2-7

Returning Injury
Novel (2009) $14.95   978-0-9746212-3-4

Blue the Bird, On Flying
Children's $6.95   978-0-9746212-1-0

ORDERING INFORMATION

AtlasBooks

www.AtlasBooks.com

Phone: 1-800-247-6553 • Fax: 1-419-281-6883

Email: info@atlasbooks.com

30 Amberwood Parkway • P.O. Box 388
Ashland, OH 44805

THE GENTLEMEN'S CLUB, A Story For All Women

ISBN: 978-0-9746212-0-3

Angie doesn't want to be a victim anymore. Deep down what she hopes for most is to find a good man to love and to feel safe in this world, but her fears take her down the wrong path. After befriending other women down on their luck, they decide to get revenge on men who go to strip clubs.

"The Gentlemen's Club had me laughing and crying, occasionally at the same time. This book made me think about the future of my daughters. There are so many issues in this book that need to be addressed. One is abuse; it is common, it can occur anywhere. The girls of today need to be protected, physically and emotionally. They need to be talked to and heard. We need to keep them on the right path, or too many of them will become a character in this novel. As the author says, women are strong and amazing and we need to support each other. We all need to read 'The Gentlemen's Club'."

—Cindy S.

"In thirty words or less, "Wow!" Everything about it, the colors, the cover says read me...I could not put the book down. Your book has changed my life. I was 48 before I was exposed to the concept that we women should be taking care of each other."

—Cara G.

"It is AWESOME"

—Shelly G.

TOUCHABLE LOVE,
An Untraditional Love Story

ISBN: 978-0-9746212-2-7

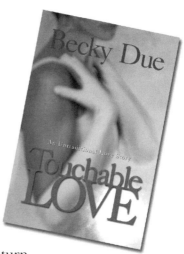

Love will always conquer fear and
Christy has much to fear. When she
enters the lives of two men, they
teach her everything she needs to
know about love. But, while dealing
with her past issues and trying to
treat her body like the temple it is,
she teaches them a thing or two in return.

*"Magnificent! Becky Due's Touchable Love is truly a gift from the
heart that will inspire, empower, transform and enrich your life with a
wisdom that we all need to embrace and remember!"*

—Debbie Friedman, M.S, C.Ht., Author,
Creator of Cleaning Out The Closet Of Your Mind
and Manifesting Made Easy,
www.cleaningoutthecloset.com

*"Touchable Love is a compelling story that moves quickly. Much
truth, highly engaging and a great read to follow The Gentlemen's
Club."*

—Bob Keeton, Living Successfully Radio,
www.livingsuccessfully.com

*"Touchable Love is an important book for women. Not only does it
confront important social issues, but also it inspires women to live
with dignity, honesty and passion."*

—Judith Smithson, Author,
Smithson's Island: The Necessity of Solitude

BLUE THE BIRD, ON FLYING

ISBN: 978-0-9746212-1-0

Blue the Bird does not want to fly. Follow Blue's journey of self-discovery. Blue is a lesson on self-esteem and independence.

My 6 year old is learning to read this year and she really enjoyed reading along with me. First I read the book to her and then she read it to me. She said, "I liked it when Blue learned how to fly, he was afraid and didn't know he could do it all by himself - but he could!" She also enjoyed going back through the book and identifying the colors and shapes on each page. Blue the Bird is also a great reminder to us adults that we can trust and rely on ourselves to succeed in life.

—Daughter loves Blue!

"I loved the message in Blue the Bird, On Flying, so I gave the book to my unmotivated 23-year-old son. He loved the book. He was inspired and motivated and I'm happy to say he now has a part-time job and has began taking classes at the community technical college. I'm not saying it was because of Blue the Bird, but its message is loud and clear to all who read it... maybe the book has a better message for young adults."

—Nancy M.

The Writers' League of Texas Recognizes Becky Due as a Teddy Children's Book Award Finalist for Blue the Bird On Flying. (November, 2007)

—Writers' League of Texas

Acknowledgements:

I want to thank everybody who is in my life or has been in my life: Women Going Forward, my college instructors, my friends, my family and every person who has helped me with my books. I especially want to thank, Scott, the love of my life.

I never thought this was possible...
I am proof that dreams do come true.

Becky Due, like the main characters of her novels, spent many years running from herself. In 1996, after a bout of being homeless, she started to pick up the pieces  of her life and worked hard to put her new life together. Through writing, Due found her passion. She has authored several books and is currently working on her next novel. In May of 2007, Due started the first national women's telephone group called "Women Going Forward."

Happily married she and Scott live in Colorado, Florida and Alberta, Canada with their two "kids" Buddy, the cat and Shorty, the pug.

Women Going Forward™

I started "Women Going Forward" for two reasons; we get stuck and we often lack the support and encouragement to get unstuck.

I know that every problem is solved by, first, acknowledging that there is one, second, finding the tools, encouragement, inspiration and support (that's where our group comes in) and third, ultimately making the decision and taking the steps to change your life.

My life and my novels are based on this principle. I was raised without a father, sexually abused when I was a child, married an abusive man and eventually found myself homeless. I was stuck in certain beliefs about myself and others. I was out of control in taking the role as a victim. I ran from bad relationship to bad relationship. I medicated the pain by using all sorts of distractions. I was in survival mode and terribly unhappy.

Once I recognized I was the common denominator, I reached out for help and made the decision to fix my life. It was challenging but one of the most important times in my life. One of the best times of my life.

It's hard to explain my life today, it seems kind of boring compared to the chaos I used to embrace. But what I can say, is that I've never laughed so much, I've never felt safer, more loved, more content, or happier than I am right now today.

Our group is not made up of counselors. We are women who have gotten through the pain. We are women who are still in pain. We are supporting and reminding each other how far we still have to go, but more importantly, how far we have come.

We are Women Going Forward and that must be the focus. All of us are strong, capable, incredible women who deserve to laugh and love and be loved and live amazing lives with all our dreams coming true! We are women coming together to help make that happen for each and everyone of us.

Join Women Going Forward every Wednesday evening at 9:15 p.m. (Eastern) by calling 1-800-391-1709 and enter the bridge code 553265. Write it on your calendar and set your cell phone alarm. It just might be the best hour you've given yourself in a long time.

You don't have to drive anywhere. You don't have to take a shower, do your hair or wear makeup. You don't even have to have a quiet house (thanks to the mute function 4 *) But you do have to be ready to spend one hour with some great Women Going Forward!

Our rules are simple: No swearing, No interrupting and No man bashing or generalizing about men in a negative way.

If you know other women who could benefit from this group please invite them to join us.

For more information, please go to www.womengoingforward.com